Eli's Journey

Life of a Scottish Immigrant's Family in the Tennessee Valley

ANTHONY WILSON

DEDICATION

This story is fictional and loosely based on historic facts surrounding the era of settlement of the Tennessee Valley. I took some liberties with historical dates to make the story better. It is set during the time span that saw the bulk of the Scottish, Scotch-Irish, (or as I prefer), Ulster Scots immigrants pour into the valley. That period was roughly 1720-1850.

I chose to write, as the characters would have spoken. The language and humor is realistic, though dry and crude at times. The Scots were people of strong faith who made strong drink, that was just the way it was, I do not pass judgment. The lives of these people were full of hard times, laughter, wars, disease, and death. The resiliency of the Scots is also present throughout the story.

The tragedies and conflicts formed these early pioneers and set the precedence for the generations to follow. These qualities are present in the valleys of East Tennessee, Virginia, North Georgia, and Western North Carolina of today. They appear in the humor, toughness, and faith that pervade these mountains and valleys.

I hope you find within these pages a story that portrays the life of the Scottish inhabitants of the mountains and valleys of the Southern Appalachians. Today, most people who live in this valley are not aware of the impact of the Scottish people; I hope your awareness will change with my humble effort, herein.

I dedicate this story to my Scottish ancestors, pioneers and patriots, who endured hard times and survived. I thank them for their sacrifices, faith, hard work, and traditions.

CONTENTS

ACKNOWLEDGMENTS

I thank God for His mercy and grace in my life and for gifting me with the most wonderful family and friends one could ever ask for, especially to my late "Granny" Mary Frances Lewis, who piqued my interest in history and family with the stories she told me when I was a boy growing up in East Tennessee.

CHAPTER ONE
MEET ELI MAGOWAN

Eli MacGowan knocked the mud from his boots and closed the door behind him. The cabin was cold, damp, and dark. Darkness filled Eli's cabin and soul, a darkness not measured by words.

He fumbled in the match tin, retrieved a match and raked it to life on the stovetop. He lit the coal oil lamp and watched it create an amber glow in the room. The interior of the cabin was now only cold and damp.

He grabbed a few pieces of pine kindling and started a fire in the stove. He mixed up some cornbread batter and sat impatiently as the cast iron skillet started to heat up.

The batter sizzled as he poured it into the hot greasy skillet. He laid two pieces of bacon to the side of the cornbread cakes, flipped the cakes a few times and threw them onto his tin plate.

It felt good to sit, even better to eat. The chill of the late winter day had taken its toll on his 70-year-old joints. He patted his belly and spoke, "that was good." Although there were seldom any humans around to hear him, Eli talked aloud often.

He toed the heel of one boot, eased his feet, one at a time, from their leather prisons. This revealed his toes through the openings in the end of his wool socks. He said, "I'll have to fix them dern holes one of these days."

It was not as if he didn't have the time, Eli no longer had to provide for anyone but himself. He had the time, but fixing his socks was not a priority right now.

He took a few scraps of his supper to set aside for his breakfast and handed the rest to the old dog on the front porch. Eli just called him "Dawg"; Eli was not prone to naming animals because he didn't want to make a strong attachment. There was a long line of "Dawgs" in Eli's life.

Dawg devoured the scraps of food, as Eli realized that this had become a nightly ritual for both. He patted Dawg on his old head and turned back to his chair.

He retrieved his pipe, packed it full of tobacco, lit it from the stove, with a broom straw and settled in. Eli hummed an old church hymn and thought how he missed his family and his church but his pride crept into his thoughts and he stopped humming and tried to empty his head. He puffed up the tobacco and knocked the ashes out into the stove.

Eli carried the lamp over by his bed and listened to the corn shucks crackle as he eased his old bones into the mattress. He blew out the lamp.

The cabin was dark and quiet; the quietness, only interrupted by the occasional sound of the fire popping in the stove and the logs creaking in the cabin walls in protest of the cold north wind. These sounds were welcome interruptions to the dark space that was otherwise void of any sound or light.

It was about this time at night that, when he was on better terms with The Almighty, that he would say his prayers, but not these days. Instead, most nights Eli reserved this time for thinking about Maggie. He thought about the day that Maggie talked him into spending twelve dollars to purchase the box stove. Eli, in his usual thrifty way had thought the fireplace and Dutch oven was adequate, but relented to Maggie's wishes.

As usual, Maggie was right. Maggie was right most of the time but he had failed in letting her know, that and a combination of his hardened Scottish will that was mostly to blame for his wrinkled old body sleeping alone tonight.

He and Maggie had slept in their bedroom in the big feather bed, but Eli had closed off the rooms and moved a bed into the front room, less to take care of he thought.

Eli was starting to figure out why, last summer, Maggie had moved to their oldest son Isaac's place in Calhoun. Eli could be hardheaded and prideful at times, as most people that knew him would attest.

Eli had allowed things to cause him to become a hard man. Hard, prideful, and stubborn do not mix, he thought. Although he missed Maggie something fierce, he didn't know how to get her back, on terms that would keep his pride intact.

"Well, enough thinkin' tonight", he said. Eli closed his eyes, thought about praying again but chose to just roll over and go to sleep.

After a few hours, Eli awakened, rolled over and sat up on the edge of the bed. He kept the bedcovers around him, rubbed his eyes, took a deep breath, and felt the chill in his lungs. On nights like this, Eli thought about using the chamber pot that Maggie used during the night, but he refused thinking it unmanly.

He thought long and hard about putting his feet on the cold cabin floor, but the pain in his bladder was not going away.

In the winter, he avoided the trip on the icy, cold trail to the outhouse and chose the convenience of relieving himself off the edge of the porch.

He slowly stood up and shuffled to the door, opened it, stepped over Dawg, and propped his groggy self up against the porch railing. He lifted his nightshirt and relief was soon upon him.

The moon was full and he could see the steam rising from the ground he had sprayed. He didn't tarry any longer than required, because of the cold air invading his exposed skin.

He shuffled back to the cabin, as Dawg whimpered to enter, "get in there"; Eli grumbled. Dawg didn't allow any time for Eli to change his mind and made a quick move through the door, taking full advantage of his master's generosity. Eli followed behind the old mutt and closed the door behind him.

He checked the fire, replenished the wood into its belly, and retired, hoping to sleep the rest of the night without having to visit the cold porch again. He rolled onto his side and drifted back to sleep.

Eli's eyes opened up to a dark cabin, he knew it was time to get up because the fire had almost burned out in the stove, witnessed by the cold air he was breathing. Dawg had occupied the space at the end of the bed and was snoring. Eli nudged him in his ribs and said, "Get up and put some wood in the stove." Dawg only grunted at Eli's weak attempt at humor and began to snore again.

Eli eased his feet from under the cover and sat up on the side of the bed. He rubbed the long white whiskers of his scruffy old beard and stood up. His body cracked a tune for each joint, as Eli moaned. He slipped on his breeches and shirt, shuffled over to the stove, loaded it up, sat down, and waited for his joints to thaw a bit.

Eli's stirring caused Dawg to show signs of life, briefly looking at him but he lay back down to wait for breakfast. The sun was starting to chase the darkness from the cabin. Eli thought, although there was only one window, it provided plenty of light. Maggie wanted more windows, but he thought that would encourage too much time inside. There was always plenty of work to do outside. Maybe he was right about the window after all, he thought. He squinted and realized that his eyes were getting old, he thought again that Maggie *was* right; it sure would be easier to see with another window, or two. "Oh well, time to get to work", he grunted.

Eli picked his breakfast from the plate he had left on the table, leftover cornbread and a piece of fat bacon. Dawg was up to receive his usual cornbread and bacon breakfast too.

Eli slipped on his old deer hide coat and shuffled out to the porch, stretched and headed to the barn, with Dawg in trail. Now, the barn was not just a barn; it was Eli's place of business. Eli removed the oak slat that kept the barn door secured, scraped the door across the worn grooved path the door had cut in the dirt, and entered. The barn was much larger than the cabin; it too was a handsome work of skilled construction.

The sturdy structure was three levels; the top level was where he malted his barley for his whisky. The level beneath that held tobacco, hay, corn, chestnuts and whatever needed keeping in the dry. The lowest level was where his whisky still, woodworking benches, blacksmithing furnace, stables and farm tools were located. Eli built the barn on the side of a sloped hill, which allowed the lower level access from the front and the second level access in the rear of the barn, both at ground level.

The foundation, built from carefully selected stones, and fitted to be solid. The walls were logs eight inches thick, hand-hewn chestnut, some, measuring in length up to twenty feet. Notched with precision, and dovetailed to lock in place at the corners. Chinking between the logs was sparse, due to the tight fit. All who saw this sturdy and functional building admired Eli MacGowan's skill.

Eli, although not a vain person, privately admired his work when entering the barn, but today he didn't have time for such admiration. Today was day five, which meant it was time to run his whisky. Eli walked over to the mash vat, gave it a last stir, perfect he thought.

Eli prided himself in making the best whisky in this corner of Tennessee. His father had taught him the family art of making fine Scotch whisky.

The process was unchanged through the generations, except for the lack of peat moss to filter and flavor the whisky; another modification from the old way of making MacGowan Scotch Whisky was that he didn't age the whisky, at least not most of it.

He did have a barrel or two set aside, though he rarely tapped those barrels anymore. They just set there, aging to perfection.

Eli thought this would be a fine run. He only made three runs from the slop or mash, as some called it, most others made four or five. That and fine spring water were part of the secret to his fine brew. It was much more work but Eli MacGowan was not afraid of work.

Eli thought about a conversation he had with his father and grandfather, both men founded in the faith and the teachings of the King's Bible. He asked if it was not wrong to make whisky, was it not a sin? They both pondered and his father answered, "Son is it a sin for a man to make an honest living off the things the Lord has provided?" He continued, "Is it a sin to make a gun knowing it will be used to murder, but also to provide game for the table of its owner, or keep his family safe?" He continued, "That is how it is with our whisky, it is used to help ease the pain of old men, quench a young child's cough, is that wrong?" "So, if a gun is used to murder, and if our whisky is used to assist a drunkard, both are sins but the sin is on the user, not the provider." "It is a skill that we Scots have known for generations, if it *is* a sin, I pray that the Lord will forgive us."

Eli stood pondering his father's reasoning and thoughts, remembering that the MacGowan men didn't drink the whisky, as they didn't want to cause anyone to think of them as drunkards.

Eli mumbled under his breath "Back to work."

After corking the last clay jug, Eli started packing the jugs onto the wagon, he gingerly placed a layer of hay in the bed of the wagon and set each jug and packed hay around each to safeguard his cargo from breaking. It was a rough and bumpy road ahead. He loaded the jugs from the previous whisky runs for this month, along with today's run.

With the wagon fully loaded, Eli admired his work, made one last check of his valuable cargo, and tugged the oxen into motion. "Let's go Dawg" he said and started leading the oxen and wagon down the worn trail from MacGowan Hollow towards the settlement below.

Eli made this trip every four weeks, as he had for over 10 years. He passed by the family cemetery and nodded to honor the graves of his saintly mother. Eli had brought her here, from Washington County since his father had died. He remembered how happy she was here. Eli remembered how happy he was for his mother's presence here too. Eli remembered years before his sons and brothers had helped him clear and grub this land. They built fences and cut the chestnuts for the cabin, barn, smokehouse, and springhouse. He recollected how much pride they had in their labor.

In his mind, Eli could see his mother and Maggie bringing their dinners to the field, he missed them both. A hard lump rose in his throat. Bumping along the path, he looked away before he saw the three tiny headstones next to his mother's grave, too many memories for one morning he thought.

Back to business, the wagon griped its way down the trail the three miles to the Federal Road and on to the settlement.

Eli seldom saw anyone this time of the day, and that suited him fine. He was not very sociable these days. He had buried his mother last winter, laid her beside his three children. He never spoke about his loss, it went without words, but his face told the story to anyone who would look.

The lines on his ruddy face were frequent and deep, they cut into his forehead like furrows in his spring fields. His eyes were blue and set deep behind his bushy red eyebrows. They were sad eyes that told a story of a hard, bitter, and beaten old man.

Eli tied off the ox to the rough sawn porch railing of the MacAndrews Mercantile and General Store. Eli often thought how MacAndrews had made grand plans for this little trading post, unfulfilled as of now.

Eli knew MacAndrews made a handsome profit from selling his whisky to the gold rushers over the mountains in Dahlonega. He also knew that MacAndrews would cut his fine whisky with spring water to stretch it and make more profit, but he didn't care. He never said a word about this to MacAndrews. He felt *that* was MacAndrews's business and Eli was not prone to meddling into the affairs of others. MacAndrews paid him a fair price and that was enough.

Eli raked his boots on the stone steps to separate the mud from the worn leather soles; the planks creaked as he stepped onto the porch and strolled into the store.

MacAndrews was shoving a stick of wood into the stove. It was warm inside and the warmth felt good on Eli's old joints. Eli grunted to MacAndrews, he grunted back. MacAndrews said "how many?" Eli replied "sixty four gallons".

MacAndrews hollered at his clerk, John Corntassel, a Cherokee, for the most part. He reported to the porch and began to count the jugs. This action usually caused a fire in Eli's backside, but he had learned it was just MacAndrews' way.

A family relationship existed between MacAndrews and Eli, due to the marriage of Eli's daughter, Sally to MacAndrews' nephew, John. MacAndrews stayed close to his money and didn't trust anyone, even Eli, who he had known for over 10 years.

Corntassel completed his inventory and proceeded to unload the jugs.

MacAndrews said, "How you want to take your payment?" Eli responded, "I need a sack of meal, sack of flour, jar of them peach preserves, four pokes of chewin' backer, a gallon of coal oil, and the rest in gold coin."

There was plenty of paper money issued and used these days, but Eli didn't trust it, he preferred gold, he trusted things God provided more than something man had printed.

MacAndrews started placing the order on the counter and in Eli's canvas sack. Then MacAndrews counted out the newly minted Dahlonega gold coins to fulfill Eli's payment, just as Corntassel finished loading the empty return jugs onto the wagon.

Eli opened his hand for the coins, received them, placed them his leather pouch and pulled the string closed. MacAndrews was always curious why Eli never counted the money; this ran against his nature. If nothing else, Eli was trusting and knew MacAndrews was trustworthy.

Slinging the sack over his shoulder, Eli picked up his coal oil can, grunted his farewell to MacAndrews and Corntassel and left the mercantile.

A few steps up the road Dawg, who had been busy sniffing all the other dogs in the settlement, joined Eli. What a crew this course old Scot and big wooly mongrel dog made, clinking up the road.

Most people in the settlement had become used to Eli's ways by now and just accepted his being different. They knew his circumstances and left him alone.

CHAPTER TWO
IT AIN'T OVER YET

Leading the wagon back to the cabin, reminded Eli of marching over the mountains with Colonel Sevier. It was the fall of 1780 and being a young man seeking adventure; it didn't take much for Eli to get his gear together for the fight. Talk around Watauga was that a Colonel Ferguson had threatened to hang the settlement leaders and burn their farms if they didn't swear loyalty to King George.

Well, most of the men in the valley, being sons of Scots, didn't have a warm feeling for ol' King George. The fact that he was trying to run their lives didn't do anything to improve that feeling. Never known to pass up a good fight, Eli thought this looked to be a good one.

On a frosty October morning, Eli kissed young Maggie goodbye, hugged his baby son, and headed off to war. Eli and his brother Isaac rendezvoused with the hundreds of other Overmountain Men at the Sycamore Shoals on the Watauga River.

Word had reached the leadership that two of William MacGowans sons were there. They were asked by a young lieutenant to be sergeants, although neither had any skills in leading men; word of their stock was enough.

They assigned Eli and Isaac a platoon of twenty men each. Some of the "men" were actually boys and although tough, fiery, and could shoot, most were still green and none had ever been shot at; for that matter, neither had Eli or Isaac.

After handing out the slim rations to his men, Eli stepped back and observed the throng encamped by the Watauga River. He thought how they were a ragtag bunch and wondered how many would live to see another spring.

The fall rains had turned the plowed fields around the shoals into a hog wallow. Eli's feet were muddy, cold, and wet and he soon learned to ignore this condition as it became normal for most of the thirteen days on the march.

Marching orders came and the men took to the trail. It could have been his imagination, but it seemed that the entire one hundred fifty miles to King's Mountain was uphill. The marching started as soon as you could see your feet and ended when you could not. The trail they marched was muddy, cold, and never easy. They marched until their feet became as tough as leather soles, as most didn't have boots.

The numbers grew along the march, picking up men and boys from the mountain settlements along the way. Eli and Isaac guessed they were near two thousand by the night they reached the foot of Kings Mountain in the South Carolina Upcountry.

Word passed that they would attack the Tories and Royalists who were encamped on the top of the mountain. Eli didn't know much about war but he figured they were at a disadvantage as far as geography. He knew from hunting that the high ground was better for finding and killing. The morning would tell, he thought.

They marched all night to get into their starting places for the charge. All the men were tired but ready to get the battle started and finished. Eli and Isaac were close enough to keep in eyeshot of each other; this was a comfort to both.

The officers barked the orders to advance and they all started in a trot up the mountain. The Over Mountain Men completely encircled the base of the mountain. The thoughts of all were that they would meet their fellow mountain men at the top, alive.

Eli could still hear the sounds of the Tories screaming as they died. He could smell the blood, burning wood and powder. Eli fired his long rifle and hit its mark; a frightened young man took the ball in his face and dropped. They fought their way to the top, firing, striking with the butt of rifles, or just slashing with a skinning knife. The fight was brutal but was not a long one, start to finish, it lasted hardly an hour. Eli often wondered if it was worth the walk. He later heard that Washington and Jefferson said it turned the tide in the war. Eli thought aloud, "Not gettin' killed was good too."

The victory celebration was modest, since it was the first time most of the warriors had killed a human being. Eli checked his men and was pleased that he had not lost even one.

Eli then turned his attention to Isaac; he saw a few of his brother's charge and inquired about Isaac's whereabouts. The men had a look that told Eli that the word was not going to be good.

One boy spoke and said, "He took a ball about half way up, we tried to stay and tend him but he told us to keep goin'". The boy continued; "he is about a stone's throw that way", as he pointed.

Eli was in a daze, he was in a strange place, killing men, narrowly escaping death, and now hearing that they have shot Isaac. He didn't know whether to hurry to find his brother or not, what if he is dead, he thought but what if he needs me!

Eli broke into a run down the mountain. Passing the dead and wounded, slashing through the downed limbs and trees, through the smoke and fire. Then there he was, his brother, propped against a poplar tree.

Eli shook his wounded brother, ***"Isaac, Isaac!"*** he shouted, "It's me Eli!" Isaac slowly opened his eyes and grinned at his younger brother. "I heard the yellin', figured we won" said Isaac. Eli barely whispered, "We won Isaac". Eli could see his brother had lost a considerable amount of blood and he knew from watching animals die, that it was *not* good.

Isaac weakly spoke, "Eli, tell the folks that I fought bravely and tell Mollie that I love her and will see her in heaven and Eli, bury me in a sunny place on this mountain".

Eli started to cry, his brother asked him to hold his hand. "Eli pray with me", Isaac started to pray, in a whisper, "Though I walk through the valley of the shadow of death, I'll fear no evil for thou art with me", he struggled to breathe and his eyes looked straight ahead. Eli watched Isaac pass to the next world.

Eli, still weeping, closed his brother's eyes, he picked him up and carried him to the top of the mountain and laid him on the trampled ground. He didn't see the residue of the battle, nor the end fighting still going on in spots; he found a thin flat stone to use as a shovel and started digging a grave for his brother. The men in Eli and Isaac's platoons gathered around and wept with Eli. They helped him dig.

It was a hard time.

Eli left his brother on King's Mountain that day, along with dozens of other brothers, sons, husbands, and fathers. Just simple men with a dream to live free from the tyranny of the British; they rounded up their things and Eli made one last survey of this mountain top and thought how valuable this land was, men had bled, died and been maimed for life on its account.

Eli kneeled one last time and said his final goodbye to Isaac. Just then, the sun broke through the smoky haze and shined on his brother's grave. His brother's last wish, for a burial in a sunny spot, now fulfilled; Eli wiped away a tear and headed down the mountain for home.

The return trip home was surreal, the constant sound of marching feet often broken with shouts of celebration of victory mixed with times of quiet reflection, sobbing, thinking of the loss. Eli was both excited and dreadful of reaching his valley, knowing his greeting would share equal emotions of happiness and grief.

Eli saw his first stop come into view; it was his folk's farm. William and Sarah MacGowan smiled and praised the Lord for delivering him back as they hugged him. Eli found that the words he had rehearsed on the journey from King's Mountain would not flow from his mouth. He could not speak.

His mother and father told him how happy they were that he was alive and well. His mother asked about Isaac. The look in Eli's eyes froze his mother and father with terror.

Eli's mother's voice quivered as she whispered, "Do not tell us son, I can't bear the words." William MacGowan cleared his throat and with a tremble in his hard Scottish voice said, "Son, let me hear the words that I dread."

Eli cleared his throat and with a quivering voice said the hardest words he had uttered in his young life. "Isaac fought bravely but was killed near the top; I buried him in a sunny spot on the mountain top". His mother collapsed screaming. William sat with her on the floor and wept.

Eli joined his mother and father and felt the sorrow penetrating the walls of this cabin. His mother screamed for the loss of her first-born son. The echoes of their sorrow flooded the valley. Eli's mother knew she would never see Isaac's face again, in this life.

Mollie, Isaac's young wife, had heard the news of the arrival of the returning soldiers and darted into William MacGowan's cabin to witness the scene there. Eli tearfully repeated his story to Mollie and she broke from his grasp and ran from the cabin screaming, "**No, no, no!**", until she was out of sight.

Eli's oldest sister joined the mourning and said for Eli to go to Maggie; she would tend to the folks and see to Mollie. She hugged Eli and said, "Thank God you were not killed too".

Eli left for his cabin.

Eli could still remember how happy Maggie was to see him. He could see her blue eyes and red hair as she flung the door open that day and saw him standing there. She gazed upon her strapping young husband, standing over 6 feet tall, broad at shoulders, narrow waist, and strong as an ox.

They just stood there and looked at each other. They had a look of love towards each other. This love was a love that bonds a man and woman together for life, beyond words.

She drank in his expression. He had a different look about him. The war she thought at first but she felt his heart was in pain.

She lunged at him and embraced him; he wrapped his arms around his lovely Maggie and started to weep. She pushed back and with a look of shock, inquired. "What is wrong Eli"? He could only stand and reach for her embrace again. He sobbed; she joined in and cried without knowing the reason. If Eli was broken, she was broken too.

He held baby son Isaac tightly and told Maggie of his brother's fate, she cried tears of grief for Isaac, Mollie, and his mother and father.

Isaac and Mollie had no living children. Mollie had lost three newborns to the colic. They had no more children and no one knew why, but it had left them broken people. They had a strong love and it showed in their eyes, to anyone who would look.

Eli and Isaac were close as were Maggie and Mollie. Maggie said they would give Mollie some time and go to her in the morning.

Maggie and Eli held each other especially close that night. They slept with visions and dreams. Eli dreamed of the sights and sounds of death. Maggie dreamed of being in Mollie's place in that empty bed without a husband.

In the morning they woke embracing and in love. They lay and talked. Maggie wondered how Mollie could cope with her loss. Eli said "The MacGowans will take care of her needs; she was now and would *always* be one of them". They talked more and wept together. Eli was proud he had named his son after his brother Isaac.

Maggie whispered to Eli "I am carrying another MacGowan in my belly". Eli smiled and exposed that big toothy grin and said, "This is good, more hands for the farm", and thought this *was* good news, and they sure did need some good news today. He held Maggie tight and thought this would be a hard day, but they were young and things would be better and the MacGowans would be happy in this valley again.

Dawg barked at a squirrel in a hickory tree and snapped Eli's mind back. He almost had a smile on his face, but that soon went away. Eli unhitched the ox, parked the wagon, and started his chores. He milked the cow, gathered eggs, fed the animals, and slopped the hogs. The hogs especially liked the fact that the sweet barley mash was used up, made for a good treat. He grabbed a scoop of corn for his mule. The mule started crunching; Eli thought it was a pleasant sound.

Eli had worked up a hunger today and felt he would treat himself to some biscuits and some of those peach preserves he had bartered for earlier in the day. The fresh flour would come in handy for that, yes indeed. So, he was off to cooking.

When Eli finished cooking, he sat his fine meal on the table and ate his fill, then sopped up the remains of the peach juice and butter with a biscuit, put some aside for supper along with a piece of ham he had brought from the smokehouse.

Dawg was waiting for his meal too, and Eli didn't disappoint him, tossing a biscuit and a chunk of ham his way. Dawg licked the last crumb from the floor, Eli said, "leave some for the mice, and they need to eat too." He chuckled at the expression that Dawg returned. Eli was surprised that he starting to find humor in things again.

"Well, back to work," Eli said. He headed out to the barn, retrieved his crosscut saw, axe, and headed up the hollow. He walked up the trail to where he knew a dead chestnut tree was waiting.

He sized it up and started cutting a wedge shape out of the front, to make it fall into the trail. Once Eli had cut the wedge, he laid the crosscut to the trunk of this goliath of the mountains.

Eli felt the chestnut starting to go, stepped back up the hill, and watched it slowly start to lean towards the trail. Then *it went!* Thundering to the ground, the chestnut slapped the limbs of its sibling trees. The wake created by the falling giant, tossed a large stray limb between Dawg and Eli. It slammed to the ground with a thud. Eli and Dawg looked at each other. Eli said, "That could have cracked our noggins!" Eli laughed aloud; Dawg only crooked his head in confusion.

Eli spoke, "what in the world is going on here, did I laugh again? Am I going daft?" Dawg continued to look confused.

Eli propped his big foot on the fresh chestnut stump and admired his work. He had learned this skill from his father on the farm in Washington County. It was a skill of survival; the trees had to go to make way for crops and gardens. It made the logs for the cabins, barns, churches, and schools. Nothing was wasted; he used every part of the tree, but the stump.

How many days of backbreaking work had he endured with the MacGowans toiling with axes, picks, and timber levers trying to dislodge those blasted stumps with their spider webs of roots from the ground. Eli remembered that William MacGowan didn't put much stock in leaving the stumps in the ground. Eli once mentioned that the O'Malley farm had stumps in the fields that they weaved around with their plows. His father just grunted something about them being trifling, and gave him a matter of fact look that he still remembered to this day.

William MacGowan was a hard man, from a long line of hard men. They were the progeny of men that had survived the brutality of Scotland as well as the harshness of building a life in this new land.

Hardness had served them well. Eli remembered his father

saying often that "all us MacGowans want is to be left alone, to farm our land in peace and make our whisky." He agreed with his father, thinking he would have to add, making babies, to that list. The MacGowans had taken the bible literally; the part that said to go forth and replenish the earth. A MacGowan family often had well over a dozen offspring.

Eli was no exception; he and Maggie had contributed sixteen fine youngins' to America. They had twelve sons and four daughters. He had lost count of all the grand children. He recollected that Maggie told him that Isaac was a grandpa, so he figured that made him a great grandpa. He often joked with Maggie that she should have rolled over and let him go to sleep, a few nights.

"Well, back to work", Eli said to Dawg, as he started cutting the limbs from the chestnut tree. He worked until it was too dark to swing the double bit axe without fear of splitting his skull.

Eli and Dawg eased back down the trail to the cabin. Eli stood the axe and the saw on the porch, and went inside, started a fire in the stove and sat down to his supper.

It was a quiet evening, good for thinking. Eli was doing a fair bit of that lately. He spoke, "well; I got to hitch that tree up to the oxen and drag it down to the bottom and finish cuttin' it up. Then I need to bring the limbs down too". He could not keep his thoughts in order, this was not normal for Eli; he had too much on his mind. His thoughts today were on his family, the war, his mother and father, and of course Maggie.

Then it happened, without warning, Eli started to weep; next came the loud guttural screaming and cursing at The Almighty. This emotional tirade was beyond Eli's control, it took control of his mind, soul, and body. He stood up and went onto the porch, hoping to deflect the feelings by distracting himself with the change of location.

It didn't work; he roared and screamed so loud that the people in the settlement had to hear him. They had heard this before, and several of the settlement people knew the feeling too.

Eli directed his anguish towards the three little headstones down the trail; he could still see their faint images in the dusky light. The little headstones were reminders of the cause of this pain and bitterness, which consumed this old Scot.

The Yellow Fever, in one week, took the lives of Mattie, Gwen, and thirteen-year-old Angus or Gussie, as all called him.

The settlement buried over twenty, young and old but the MacGowan family suffered the cruelest blow of all.

Pastor Emmons did his best to explain this to Maggie and Eli; it worked somewhat for Maggie but Eli would not allow God off the hook. He would hold God responsible for his loss, from that day and would not hear otherwise.

Maggie suffered from the loss of her three youngest children but seemed to manage, but she could not manage the loss of Eli. He was a stranger to her from that day. He became bitter and dark. Life held no flavor for him, he sought darkness and longed for his father's wisdom, but he too, was in the ground, beside his three precious children.

His mother soon lost her will to live. She was in constant grief over her darling babies and her son's bitterness. Eli often heard her pray and cry herself to sleep. Then one morning they found her cold body in bed; she was gone too.

All the MacGowans and neighbors present wept as they laid his mother in the cold ground beside little Gussie, Gwen, and Mattie.

The sound of Amazing Grace echoed down the valley as Eli held back his tears and played his bagpipes. It was his last gift to his mother. Eli regretted not laying his mother beside his father in Washington County; it was too far to carry her body. It was a comfort to him though to know his mother would always be close by.

It was a hard time.

Now Maggie was alone, she had lost her only shoulder to lean on, because Eli had long ago taken his shoulder away from everyone.

Eli remembered arriving one evening to a dark cabin; a strange chill filled its space. He lit the lamp and saw a note scratched on the table with a piece of charcoal. The words explained the chill, Maggie had written, "Eli, I love you too much to see you this way, I'll be at Isaac's".

The words burned him to his core, it hurt, but it was for the best he thought. He sank to the cabin floor. Maggie was gone. Eli was alone with his bitterness. Well, there *was* Dawg, but he was not much in the lines of consoling.

"Glad to have that out", Eli spoke to Dawg. He had endured another "spell of rage", as Maggie called it. He took a deep breath and shuddered.

Still angry, Eli looked up to the stars and pointed his big finger. He directed his comments to God and yelled *"it ain't over yet"*. Eli stood and heard his words echo through the valley. He shuddered again and went into the cabin.

CHAPTER THREE
THE OLD SCOTS

Eli lay down, closed his eyes, and his dreams overtook him, the kind of dreams you wake up the next morning and remember.

He was back at his mother and father's cabin. Eli was a young boy of twelve he looked around the room and saw his brothers and sisters. There was his granny Gillian [Gull e an] MacGowan too, or as Grandpa Angus MacGowan called her, Gullie. She was a spry woman, full of mischief and laughter.

Widowed for two years or so, was Granny Gullie. Eli was always mesmerized to listen to her tales of adventure on the Atlantic and her talk of her homeland in the Highlands of Scotland.

Eli often wondered what an American *was*. The Watauga community in the Upper East Tennessee Mountains was made up of Scots, Irish, Cherokee, English, German, Dutch, African slaves and who knew what else.

Eli heard from his father, at an early age, that expectations for MacGowans and Scots were high. Among those expectations were to be independent and hard working. He believed in the standard they had set and strived to make his parents and grandparents proud of their name, which he carried proudly, through his life. The expectations would be the same for the name he passed on to his children and grandchildren.

Eli's grandparents, to him, were the last remnants of old Scotland in this country. They were proud but didn't express that pride; they always talked and lived a humble lifestyle. They kept some traditions alive but wanted their children woven into the fabric that was America.

He remembered how they would speak Gaelic to each other but forbid their children to speak the ancient language. This was a new country and they expected Eli and his siblings to speak like Americans.

Granny Gullie did have tales to tell. Eli often spent evenings in conversation with her. He was hungry to learn as a young lad and she was a wealth of information. Eli, being the youngest son of William MacGowan, was her favorite. She was special to Eli too.

Angus MacGowan and Gillian Munro were both born in a loosely clustered village near the high mountains and Loch Ericth. The village of Dalwhinnie, which was Gaelic for meeting place, lay between Loch Ericht and Glen Truim.

Dalwhinnie had an inn that provided lodging for the drovers moving their cattle herds to sell in Crieff. Some days the cattle would number in the hundreds as they stirred dusty clouds on their final journey to fill the bellies of the wealthy Englishmen and Lowlanders.

William MacGowan and Argyle Munro could see the budding relationship between William's son Angus and Argyle Munro's daughter Gillian. They would often wink at each other as they watched the two sitting together at church.

Granny Gullie began, "Yes Eli, we were in love. Your grandfather Angus was a strong lad and cut a fine look as he worked the fields of the MacGowans."

"We had a hard life there, living off what peat we could sell and milk, butter, and bread when the wheat crop came in. We would have fresh meat if my brothers or father killed a partridge in the meadows or killed a doe in the forest. We were happy, for the most part, and were seldom hungry."

She continued her story, as Eli sat enthralled by her words, "I remember the day Angus asked for my hand, I knew it was comin' due to my blabby sister tellin' me she had heard him ask me father."

She smiled without covering her mouth, which Eli thought was odd. Gullie always covered her mouth to prevent the world knowing about her lack of teeth, must have been ashamed of her condition, he thought. Eli didn't make much of this, he knew the beauty within his grandmother and thought she must have been a prize in her younger days; he smiled and concentrated on her words as she continued.

"One sunny day, Angus and I strolled up the stony slopes of the high mountain to the summit at Gael Charn. Eli, from here you could see the world. Loch Ericht looked like a shimmerin' sword layin' in the glen below."

"Angus had cut some heather from the moor on the way up the mountain; I wondered why he didn't give them to me as he had always before." She said.

"He bowed to a knee and said these words that I shant forget, Eli." Angus said, "Gullie, I have no ring to give you but I ask for you to be me wife," Gullie said, "He placed the ring of heather upon my wrist and waited with a solemn look, for my words."

"I said to Angus with a smiling face and with tears in my eyes, that there was no gold in all of Scotland that would mean as much as this heather band on my wrist, I shall always be by your side, will bear you many sons, and love you until the day I close my eyes forever."

Gullie continued, "One of the first things we bought in this country was a Bible." She turned and opened a chest and pulled out the family Bible. She opened the back cover and took out a yellowed piece of linen, opened it and showed Eli the dry pressed heather band that Angus MacGowan had presented her on that day long ago in the old country.

Eli watched a tear wind its way down a furrow in her face; her eyes now closed as her body and soul were on that mountain in the Highlands with her beloved Angus.

Eli allowed her to pause and waited for the story to continue. Gullie opened her eyes and cupped Eli's ruddy face in her weathered palms, held him for a few moments, and smiled.

She continued. "Angus said he didn't have much to give to a marriage, and I said I am poor too Angus but we will make it as our mothers and fathers have done for generations here in the Highlands."

Gullie's expression changed to a serious state as she said "Eli that is when your grandfather told me of his plans for our future."

Angus said, "Gillian Munro when we are man and wife, I plan to get us to America. I have heard from the soldiers passing through the village that there is land there for the taking, and I plan to take my share, if you will go with me."

Gullie spoke with astonishment in her voice to her grandson, "Eli, I was in the same time thrilled and feared to death as what Angus had said, but I told him I would step by his side all the way to America, if that was his thinkin'."

"I remember askin' Angus where America was, thinkin' it was just over the mountains or somewhere close by," said Gullie.

She said, "Angus laughed so hard I thought his kilt would drop off. He said, "No Gullie, America is a whole nuther land across the waters, we will have to get the fare and go to Edinburgh, get a ship and sail to a new land."

"Eli, I didn't know what to say, as a journey to a new land on a ship, across the waters was never in my young mind. I just smiled and took his huge hand and kissed him and said fine, when do we leave, Angus?"

Eli's grandmother continued, "Angus told me that the military was building a road to the Ruthven Barracks a few miles away and that he and his brothers and father planned to leave in the morning to seek wages for their labor."

She said, "We strolled hand in hand down the mountain, planning how we would marry and go to America. We saw a Golden Eagle circle over us and fly off to the west, Eli said that was a good sign, I didn't understand signs and only felt he was right in the matter."

Gullie said, "It seemed no time had passed when we were greeted by the MacGowan and the Munro families as well as the pastor. It was pretty clear that word had spread of Angus' nuptial plans."

"Everyone hugged and kissed us as we made our rounds from one family to the next. It was one of the days of my life that I shall never forget, Eli," Gullie said with a smile, no teeth and all.

Gullie continued, "The next morning Angus, his father William, brothers Liam and Ian walked 9 miles to the south and talked to a man about working on the military road to the Ruthven Barracks. The road was to be used to move the king's soldiers around to keep a watch on the Highlands after the Jacobite War. The Barracks didn't give us a good feeling and showed us all that we didn't live in a free land."

"It didn't take but one glance at the stout build on the MacGowans for the man to hire them all." Gullie smiled and continued, "Angus was paid real wages for the first time in his life and labored hard and saved every schilling he earned to pay for our passage to America.

Gullie said, "After the road was finished, Angus knew our time had come to leave the Highlands and go to America. He had planned to leave with his two brothers and their wives but when the time came, they didn't come but bought land with their earnings."

Gullie told Eli about the hardship of the family that remained in the Highlands after Angus and her left. She spoke angrily, "We suspected that the land that was bought by Angus' brothers were later taken as the Lowlanders took the land and moved all the Highlanders to Ulster in the north of Ireland so they could graze their sheep on the lands that our ancestors had fought, bled, and died for."

She said with a quivering voice, "We never heard from our families, only word we had was from the newcomers to the valley telling of the Removal and of the harsh life in Ulster."

Gullie continued, "We were married in the stone church that our families had entered for tens of generations before us. For as long as anyone could remember, the humble space inside the hard walls was a place for christenings, weddings, and funerals. We said our vows in the mornin' spent the rest of the day in celebration of the union of the Munro and MacGowan families. They was plenty to eat, which was rare indeed, my son."

"Angus' brother Liam let us use his cottage for our honeymoon," said Gullie. Eli's grandmother interrupted the story as she cleared her throat when Eli inquired about the term "honeymoon." There was no response from Gullie and she quickly continued.

"Two days later we gathered our meager belonging and said our tearful goodbyes and tried to keep our sadness within, it is the Highland way Eli. Just before we started, William handed Angus a leather pouch that held his earnings from working on the road, he said your brothers put a few coins in there; mind the Lord and keep the MacGowan name pure, my son, then he turned and left, never to see his son again," she said.

Eli sat mesmerized as he listened to the wise old woman speak. Gullie continued, "The MacGowan name being kept pure was mór" she paused, remembering her rules about speaking Gaelic, and said "it was big to Angus's father and Angus knew he would have to work hard to be worthy of his clan's sacrifice."

She continued, "Angus did keep the MacGowan name in good stead in this new land, it was a heavy burden for your grandfather, one he fulfilled." Gullie paused and proudly smiled.

Eli tried to picture in his mind, the journey. Gullie said, "We said our farewells, cried and hugged our families one last time." "We knew we would never see them again in this life, it was a hard day indeed." "We carried our belonging slung over our shoulders and walked with a purpose through the glens and woods of the Highlands."

"The journey began with a first step, followed by more steps that turned into miles; I felt familiar with the places along our trip on the first day but started to see new things on the second day forward."

"We had to walk the seventy-five miles to get to Edinburgh. One of the travelers we passed told this distance to Angus on the second day." Gullie continued, "We walked by day and slept in the woods by night, a blanket and Angus was my only shield from the world that neither of us had ever seen."

"We had not been beyond the glen we were born to and I was a feared most of the way, and thought of turnin' back, except Angus would not have stood for that", she smiled and continued.

Gullie described passing by the white stonewalls of Blair Castle, crossing the River Spey, River Tay, and walking along the foot of the highest mountains in all of Scotland. She talked of Stirling and following the River Forth to the edge of Edinburgh.

"We just kept puttin' our feet down until we came to edge of Edinburgh." "It was the first city we had seen, there were people thick as fleas, and the stench was beyond words, my son, beyond words. We didn't want to tarry long in this town, only long enough to find our ship."

Gullie continued, "The next morning we walked into the great city of Edinburgh, the home of kings and other great men. It was a place of old and new. A place of derelict buildings and grand new homes rising from the high ground overlooking the River Forth and the port of Leith."

"I remember when Angus pointed to the port with the great ships waiting to take us Scots to America. With much inquiry he learned where to go and who to see about our passage." She said.

A frown crept across her brow and she continued. "Eli, the city is no place for people; they become like feral dogs and have no respect for their fellow men."

"When we saw the man about our passage, he said our fare would be eleven pounds apiece. We only had thirty three pounds and had to buy supplies and land upon arriving in America."

Her voice became loud and angry as she continued," Angus had heard the fare would be nine pounds and felt this was a fair price. He worked hard and bargained the man down to ten pounds." "The grumpy old man told us we could take that or take passage on the prison ship; Eli would not subject me to that humiliation and agreed to the ten pound fare, reluctantly."

Gullie's voice softened as she continued her tale to her grandson, Eli. "We waited for two days before the ship was adequately filled; over two hundred sad and fearful faces boarded the huge vessel."

"We sailed out of Edinburgh on a cloudy day, and we hoped to see the sun shine as we headed to America. We found our spot and settled in for the ordeal, it *was* an ordeal Eli, it is a vision I shall never forget. We were packed into the ship like cord wood." She said, "We were stacked nearly on top of each other. The filth we lived in on the ship was beyond words."

Gullie paused, and then continued, "The journey was harsh, long, and cold. We were sick from the steady heaving of the ship on the black cold water; we were terrified of never reaching America alive."

Then a smile washed over her face, "I can hear the sounds of the cheering Scots, a foul smelling lot we were on that day; the day we saw America for the first time."

Eli watched as a tear trickled down his sweet Granny Gullie's face. "The creaking old ship sailed into the Chesapeake Bay." Gullie described in detail to the wide-eyed Eli. Her voice cracked as she continued the description. "It was green land," she said as she closed her eyes "except for the water, it was brown as the dirt along the shore."

Her worn face smiled as she continued, "there were tears, hugs, praying, and shouting for joy, we had survived!" Eli thought the emotions must have been beyond measure; the joy of reaching America, and the fear of the unknown that still awaited this young couple.

They were truly on their own, with all their possessions in the bags slung over their shoulders. They used almost every schilling they possessed to purchase land and supplies and headed with several hundred other Scots to their new life in a new called Virginia.

The second leg of the odyssey began as Gullie and her young husband gripped the handcart and took the first steps of their overland journey to the heart of this new land. Gullie described how she and Angus found their place in the procession and headed west. "We pulled our squeakin' handcart with our meager belongings, over 200 miles over rough trails, wadin' rivers, creeks, and fightin' the elements every hard step. We walked the trail along the James River to the Fluvanna River to the foot of the Jackson Mountain." She paused recollecting the details and continued. "The trip took over a month and we were near wore out when we arrived that late spring evenin'."

Gullie said, "It rained that night, as it had several of the days and nights along our journey, but this was different. This rain was falling on our land. It was a sweet rain indeed."

Gullie continued, "The mornin' came, your grandfather unpacked the axes, and we started to work. Being a stout built woman, I had to work as hard as the men did. I could swing an axe, pull a saw, and grub stumps."

"We knew we had a large task ahead. We had to clear the land, get the crops in, and build a cabin; and we had to complete the work before the winter snow flew", said Gullie.

Gullie's eyes closed as she continued. "Winter came early that first year and it was a hard cold winter. We managed to build a two-room cabin with hard work and the kind help of neighbors. The cabin was warm, most of the time, which was good because I was carrying your father."

Eli's father, William MacGowan was born in the spring of 1723 in America. He was the first of the MacGowans born in this new land. He had strong ties to Scotland due to carrying his grandfather William's name.

Gullie spoke, "William had to learn to work as soon as he could walk because we needed every hand we could get to clear land and make crops." Gullie beamed, "William was not alone for long, and I had a child every year for the next nineteen years."

Gullie spoke with pride when she talked of her youngins. "Fourteen sons and five daughters, I gave Angus," she said. She grew quiet for a few moments and sadness crept across her face; Eli knew that Angus and Gullie had lost a daughter and three sons to the influenza. It was a hard time.

Gullie said, "We loved the valley in Virginia, but your grandfather heard of land to be had in the Watauga Valley to the south and a few years later he and some fellow Scots journeyed to the south and purchased larger tracts of land in this fertile valley. He said we would sell and prosper more with more land, so we packed up and moved to Watauga."

Gullie smiled as she relayed the trip to Eli, "We journeyed down Holston's River and crossed over the mountains into this new valley, and it was much the same as Virginia, only more open land for the takin'."

"We had a few run-ins with the Cherokee at times; for the most part we got along. Life was hard work and more hard work, as idleness would lead to hunger," she said with a smile.

Hard work and frugality had allowed Angus and Gullie to

acquire several hundred acres of valley and mountain land, to divide among their eleven living sons. The expectation was that the four daughters would marry into land and they all did.

William, being the oldest, inherited the best land, grand bottomland near the Watauga River. That was the way of the old Scots.

Eli knew the pickings would be slim by the time he was old enough to gain his inheritance. He also knew that there was plenty of good land still left in this country and he would find his place when the time came.

Dawg loudly grunted and startled Eli from his dreamy visit with his Granny Gullie. Eli grunted back at Dawg and rolled over to return to sweet slumber, he hoped.

CHAPTER FOUR
MEETIN' MAGGIE JOHNSON

Sleep didn't come again and Eli didn't linger too long to thrash around in bed. So, he opened his eyes to the glimmering sight of a new day through the solitary window. Time to rise, he thought, and he did, after all there *was* work waiting.

After breakfast, it was off to finish with the chestnut tree. He yoked up the oxen and led them up the side of the ridge, tied them off and started to work.

For seventy, Eli could still make the chips fly. He could work as hard as most men in their twenties, for a short while, anyway.

Living alone now and without any of his sons to help, he had no choice in the matter. That suited him fine; lately he felt when he was alone, that he was in good company.

He cut the tree into six sections about eight feet each. This would make it manageable for the oxen to pull down the ridge. He bound the larger limbs into bundles with ropes; they would make good wood too. The oxen made the work easy, just eight trips to transport the logs and limbs to the wood yard.

Eli picked out a few good straight sections to build a set of chairs. That would keep him busy during rainy days, he thought. Eli rubbed his belly and looked at Dawg and said, "My guts are growlin', let's eat." Dawg showed his vote by heading toward the cabin.

After a pork tenderloin, biscuits, and coffee dinner, he was ready to cut the firewood. With maul and wedges, he split the logs to a more manageable size, laid them into the cross rack and cut the firewood. He stacked the wood in the barn to cure. This would keep his bones warm next winter he thought.

He sat on the bench to grind the edge back on his axes and it started to rain. The rain spattering on the cedar shakes sounded good to his ears. The sound reminded him of lying in bed with Maggie back in Watauga, so young and so in love. He remembered the first time he saw her.

Maggie Johnson came to the Watauga Valley the summer Eli

turned fourteen. A pair of wagons rolled past the field where Eli and his father and brothers were working, planting corn. Maggie's father stopped to ask Eli's father about how to get to the MacGowan Place. His father chuckled and said, "you are standin' in the middle of it right now sir."

Maggie's family had moved in from Bent Mountain in Virginia. Her father was the youngest son and desired a little more land on which to raise his young family. He had purchased eighty acres from his older brother, who was moving to lands in Ohio.

My father shook hands and said, "My name is William MacGowan." Maggie's father smiled and said, "My name is James Johnson; I am a younger brother to your neighbors Johnson." They talked about property lines, land quality, water and so on.

Eli was distracted from the conversation by a commotion at the wagon, he watched as it emptied out like a swarm of yellow jackets. There must have been twelve or fourteen children.

Eli's father said, "Eli, go fetch some water for them!" as he pointed to the swarm around the wagon. Eli left for the springhouse, immediately. He filled the oak bucket with cool spring water and grabbed the hollowed out gourd dipper. Eli arrived at the wagon with bucket and dipper in hand. He held the bucket so each could dip out a gulp.

There she was; the prettiest thing Eli had ever seen. Big blue eyes set in a freckled face, hair that rivaled the red glow of a perfect summer sunset. She smiled and softly said, "My name is Maggie."

Eli didn't have a response, but to stare at the water bucket and shuffle his big bare feet in the dusty ruts of the wagon road.

Maggie softly said, "Ain't you got a name boy?" Eli finally managed to look at her and stammer, "Eli, Eli MacGowan, this is *our* place." As he waved his arms in a grand gesture that, Eli thought, would certainly impress the young lady.

She said "looks like we will be neighbors; maybe I'll see youin's at church Sunday?" Eli only grinned and said, "We will be in the second, third, and fourth pews."

James Johnson returned to the wagon and said "youngins git

in the wagon." He then turned and sized up Eli and grinned. "Are you one of William's boys?" He asked.

"I'm Eli, the youngest son." They shook hands, "good to make your acquaintance, Eli MacGowan." "We will see you again, after we are settled."

Eli had not shaken hands with anyone but the preacher on Sundays; it made him feel like a grown man.

James Johnson slapped the leather against the rumps of the oxen team. The wagons jerked into motion. Maggie pulled the cover of the wagon back and peeked at Eli. Did she smile at me, he wondered. Eli smiled and watched the wagon disappear in a dusty trail over the rise and out of sight.

"Do I need to bring the strap to you boy or are you goin' to get back to work?" Eli heard his father say in his thick Scottish brogue.

Eli snapped around, walked briskly to the fields, and returned to the corn planting. Maggie would not leave his head or his dreams for the rest of the week; Sunday could not come to fast for him, he thought.

Sunday meant bathing, on Saturday night. This time, Eli didn't mind, he wanted to be his best when he saw Maggie again. He bathed and put on his clean nightshirt and off to sleep, to dream of Maggie.

Morning came; Eli put on his best clothes and combed his hair. He wanted to look his best for this Sunday. He even scrubbed the valley dirt from between his toes, since he didn't have shoes; he wanted to look his best.

The wagon trip to the Watauga Valley Church was slower than usual that Sunday, or at least it seemed that way to Eli. The old road had deep ruts, from the hundreds of trips made by the good Christians, in the valley, over the years.

Finally, they were there, Eli jumped from the wagon ahead of his sisters. His mother made note of this action and quickly corrected this deed by firmly grasping Eli by the ear. This was her method of gaining a child's attention at times. Eli had felt it more times, than he could remember, but today it seemed more harsh than usual.

Eli took his place in line and his folks led the youngins into this shrine, to our Lord and Savior. As he entered, he started to crane his neck around, to see if the Johnsons were there already. No luck, maybe they would be there before services started.

William MacGowan was a man who believed in being on time, to the point of always being early, today was no exception.

Eli waited.

Every opening of the squeaking door caused Eli's head to pivot around for a quick look at Maggie Johnson. Every head pivot caused him to feel the wrath of his mother. She not only had mastered the art of lobe stretching, she could also pinch a blue spot on ones leg. His mother was practicing pinching on Eli for turning to observe every entry into the church. This was not acceptable and Eli knew this well. He figured it was worth the pain to see Maggie.

Finally, the Johnson clan arrived and Eli caught a glimpse of Maggie. She was truly a sight to see. Her blue plaid dress showed the contours of her young figure. This sight caused Eli's heart to thump so loud and he prepared for his mother's pinch. It was an *exceptionally* long pinch, "eyes to the front laddie," she said. Well, at least his pounding heart was *his* secret, he thought.

The Johnsons were in the back of the church; Eli stole a peak a couple of times and caught Maggie looking at him.

The sermon could have been on hellfire and brimstone or the evils of whisky. Although preaching on the latter would have been risky for the preacher in *this* congregation. Eli didn't recall a word of the pastor's presentation to the congregation that day. His mind was elsewhere for sure.

"*Amen.*" Said the congregation and all turned to leave. Eli broke for the door. "Whoa there laddie," he heard his mother say as she clamped onto his arm. He sensed this was not going to have a desirable outcome and he was right.

"Since you are in such a *hurry*, why don't you take a seat right *here*," his mother whispered into his ear as she pushed him into the pew. "*You* may leave when all of the others are gone," she said.

Finally, the last old woman shuffled to the front and gave her usual lengthy commentary on the preacher's sermon of the day. *Finally*, the preacher helped her down the steps and Eli could leave the church.

The preacher turned to Eli and spoke. "What are we in such a rush about Eli?" Eli barely heard his words as he saw Maggie step up into the wagon.

She turned and smiled at him and he felt his face go crimson. Eli eventually came out of his stupor, smiled back, and waved goodbye.

"*Son, Son*, is you listenin' to me," the preacher inquired in a stern tone. Eli responded, "Yes sir."

"I noticed the lack of attention to my sermon today young Eli. You have not accepted the Lord have you?" he asked. "No sir, but I 'm thinkin' about it most of the time." said Eli.

The preacher smiled and said, "That is good, I'll continue to pray that you accept the Lord. You may go now Eli, your family is waiting."

Eli was fully aware that he had lied to the preacher, his only thoughts this day was on Maggie and not the Lord. He hoped that he could straighten that out next Sunday.

His heart sank when he saw the Johnson's wagon pull away and grow smaller in the dust of the road.

Eli heard his father say, "Get in the wagon lad." His mother only flashed lightning bolts from her eyes at him; he knew there was more to come later.

He sank into his spot in the wagon. His sisters were giggling, more than the silly girls usually did. "*What?*" Eli asked, they only giggled more. Then finally, his younger sister Annie said, "We saw you lookin' at Maggie Johnson."

"Mind your pints and quarts and *leave me be*," said Eli.

"Eli!" He heard his mother shout from the front of the wagon. "I have told you that we do not say that in *this* family. That is *not* Christian talk; *that* is drunkard talk."

"Where did you hear that?" his mother inquired.

William MacGowan looked hopefully at Eli, silently praying that the reply from his son would not include the mention of his name.

Eli thought, "Grandpa Angus said it all the time Ma." His mother looked suspicious and replied, "Well, that is drinkin' talk and will not be spoken by my youngins', you hear me lad?"

Eli only replied, "Yes ma'am;" he knew his mother would add this to his misbehavior in church and she would make a collection from his hide later.

William only winked at his son and deep down admired his shrewdness in this tricky situation. The tension was broken upon the arrival of the MacGowan wagon at its destination.

Eli was normally only thinking about Sunday dinner. Mostly his Granny Gullie's fried chicken and biscuits but today he only had thoughts of Maggie Johnson.

Eli's mother turned around and said to the wagonload of MacGowan children, "I expect best behavior today, we will be havin' company for dinner."

Eli thought not the preacher *again*, for Sunday dinner; he would certainly have another sermon directed at him about his lack of salvation, after he ate his fill of Granny's fried chicken, of course.

As they drew near home Eli could see a wagon, yep it was the Johnsons. His mother had invited them to Sunday dinner! Eli's mood instantly changed, to the good.

There stood Maggie in the middle of the Johnson swarm; her red hair peaked out from under the edges of her blue bonnet. Eli strolled up to the fringe of the Johnsons and waited. Maggie broke from the group and they both leaned up against the rail fence that ran along the road. She smiled and he smiled back.

Eli noticed his young sister, Annie MacGowan, lurking about to spy on the two. Eli slung his head at her, to motion her to leave, but she persisted. Eli wanted to talk but knew Annie would be giving a word account of the entire transaction. He pointed for her to leave and gave her a look that she *knew* carried consequences later, should she not comply. Annie took the warning from her brother and eased towards the cabin, barely out of earshot of Maggie and Eli.

Maggie spoke, "I saw you at church today, and you look nice." "So do you" Eli said. Maggie smiled; Eli felt his heart pounding again. This was strange to him, he had usually wanted to chunk rocks at all the girls, but this was not a rock chunkin' feelin', he thought.

Eli talked about subjects he knew, "your place is some good land, makes good crops, if we get rain when we need it." Maggie said, "This valley is sure pretty, I like it better than where we lived up the valley." "Not as crowded," she said.

Eli asked, "How old are you?" Maggie replied sweetly, "fourteen." Eli said, "I'm fourteen too, will be fifteen in a month." Many words filled the brief time they shared.

Eli thought he could listen to Maggie talk about anythin'; her sweet voice reminded him of the doves cooing in the cove. He just stood there a gangly oversized fourteen-year-old boy feeling love for the first time.

Eli's father stepped around the corner of the cabin and yelled "*Eli*." He motioned for them to come. Eli was startled and almost fell into the road. Maggie laughed and asked, "Are you alright?" Eli blushed and snapped straight up and tried to act as if nothing had happened, without responding.

His father shouted again "Eli, we're waitin." Eli thought how rude his father was for interrupting the sweet sound of Maggie's voice.

Maggie smiled and said, "We better go." She wanted to hold his hand and he hers. Neither could be that forward, especially on a Sunday and out of the sight of their folks. Separately they joined the rest of the Johnsons and MacGowans at the plank table under the old white oak tree. Eli sat next to Maggie, and he planned, in his heart, to be as close to her as he could, for the rest of his life.

Eli could feel the warmth of Maggie's smile as they ate. There was just somethin' especially pretty about watchin' Maggie eatin' Grannies fried chicken, he thought. Eli remembered nearly eating his weight several times at that table. This probably contributed to his considerable size and strength; he was the biggest and strongest fourteen-year-old boy in the valley, without a doubt. He could feel the summer breeze blowing down the valley. He remembered that spot was always a cool shady place to take Sunday dinner in the summer. Mmm, Grannies fried chicken.

The cow mooed and brought Eli back from his daydream. He rubbed the back of his neck, rose to fetch the milk bucket. He didn't mind milking but it was one of Maggie's chores, and she was much better at the task. The old brown Guernsey cow still didn't look too happy about the touch of Eli's rough old hands. He pulled the stool up under the udder and started milking.

The cow turned around and looked at Eli again. He said, "It's either me or bust your bag old girl." The cow snorted and turned back to munching on her grain.

Out of the corner of his eye, he saw the fat calico tomcat sneak out of the loft for his dish of milk. Eli poured the warm milk into the wooden bowl nearby. The cat purred as he drank the milk.

Dawg observed this transaction and although not happy about it, he had learned to leave the cat alone. Maggie had broken Dawg's habit of chasing the cat around the barn, after a few whacks across his nose.

The cat, like all animals on the MacGowan place served a vital purpose. His job was to keep the mice and rats out of the barn.

A large black snake kept the mice at bay around the place too, but he was scarce in the winter months. Eli figured he was holed up somewhere waiting for warmer weather.

Dawg kept the possums, foxes, gopher rats, and raccoons away from the buildings as well as helping with the hunting. Sometimes he was company for Eli, but not so much, lately.

CHAPTER FIVE
CHURNING THROUGH A WAR

Eli took the fresh milk to the cabin; let it sit for a while as he cleaned up. He tried to recollect how long the cream had been in the churn, over a week he thought, "Well I reckon it's time to churn," He said to Dawg.

He poured the day's milk into a clean gallon bucket, covered it with a clean cloth and placed a leather string around the cloth to secure it to the top of the bucket. He carried the bucket of milk to the springhouse, to sit and let the cream rise.

Eli took the top off the churn, sniffed, and looked to be sure it was in a properly soured condition. He was satisfied it was and hoisted the clay churn, with over a week's cream inside, from the springhouse. He carefully carried it back down the trail and up the steps into the cabin. He sat it in the pantry, a cool room in the cabin.

Keeping the churn cool was very important to making good cream; Eli could hear Granny Gullie say "the colder the cream the better the butter." He grinned, closed the pantry door, and returned to the springhouse to retrieve his milk for supper. As he closed the door to the springhouse, he thought how some cornbread and milk would make for a good supper tonight.

After supper, Eli took the lamp and went to retrieve the churn from the pantry. He raised the churn lid and checked its level, it was about half full, "just right", Eli said.

Churning was not one of his favorite things to do because it required Eli to sit in one place for a good spell. He thought it was worth the torture to have good fresh Guernsey butter and buttermilk. He hoped the cream was ready; maybe the process would only take an hour or so to separate the cream into butter and buttermilk.

He raised the churn top, slid the plunger up through the hole in its center, and placed the lid back into its seat.

The rhythmic up and down motion began. The sound for some reason brought back memories of the steady cadence of a marching army. Eli thought back on his second involvement in war.

It was in the fall of 1813 and the valley was on fire because of talk of Indians invading or even worse, the British. The young men were ready to defend the valley; the old men, including Eli, hoped the talk would die down, before his sons joined this war.

Eli's hope died, as the young men lined up and volunteered for the fight in Andy Jackson's army. Eli's sons were no exception; they felt they had to protect the valley from the impending invasion from the south. Eli knew he was too old, but volunteered anyway. He soon discovered he was far from the oldest man in this volunteer army.

He did have experience in killing men and most of the younger volunteer soldiers were sons of the old men who had fought in the War for Independence. The younger men looked to the wisdom and experience of the "white hairs." Eli figured if Generals White, Cocke, and Jackson, all men of advanced age, could handle this campaign, so could he.

So, on a cold frosty morning, with a substantial army assembled, Jackson marched the Tennessee Volunteers down the valley to engage the warring Hillabees and Creeks.

Eli was now a lieutenant. Eli chuckled and said to his oldest son Isaac, "Lieutenant MacGowan, I guess not many soldiers have been promoted from sergeant to an officer. I figure they put me in charge of this mounted infantry unit, mainly because I have some war experience and me and all my neighbors came on horseback!"

They marched with General White to the Mississippi Territory. This army, compiled of a large contingent of Scots and Cherokees was an impressive force. Eli thought that they would crush anything in their path, for sure.

The mostly volunteer army cleared a path over mountains and crossed cold rivers, swollen with early winter rains. Eli and the rest of the East Tennessee Valley brigade, under the command of General James White, surrounded a Hillabee village.

It was clear to Eli and his sons and anyone who would see that there was no evidence of resistance by the Hillabees. A battle ensued, with a large group of Cherokees carrying out most of the killing, as most of the valley men backed off to allow the Hillabees to surrender.

Eli remembered how the fight was brutal and bloody, as over sixty Hillabees died. With control finally gained, women and children, numbering over two hundred became prisoners of the invading army. The volunteers didn't have any causalities, due to the one sided nature of the fight.

The celebration was mostly by the young volunteers, having their first taste of war, and the Cherokees. The celebrating was subdued when this attacking army heard news that General Jackson had already accepted the surrender of this group of Hillabees the day before. The terms of surrender were in route this very day to the Hillabees.

It was now clear to Eli why the Hillabees were in disbelief of the vicious attack carried out against them. Eli was sickened at the thought and regretted his part in this unnecessary slaughter.

Eli quietly said to his sons and neighbors, "Men we have been part to a massacre today. It is not our fault, or the fault of our leaders; they just carried out the orders given, as did we."

Eli's son, Isaac, said, "Paw I am sick to death about what I have seen here today. I have seen people murdered in the name of war." Many of the others nodded in agreement and looked hollow eyed and ill.

Eli said, "I know, I feel the same, there is nothin' that we can do, we just followed orders men. Try to put it to rest tonight and eat your rations, if you have the stomach." Eli like most of the others had no appetite, which was just as well, since rations were thin anyway.

Eli knew this action would light a fire under the Hillabees. He was right; fighting was fierce for the duration of their enlistment. He felt no pride in this fight, he soon figured out the purpose of this war, it was about land and power, not for independence like the war he fought with General Sevier.

Eli thought how everyone was losing interest in this war. They didn't see the Indians as a serious threat to the valley. Morale was low, rations were even lower and hunger and cold ruled the day.

They were hunters and could kill enough game for meat but they needed more than meat to fight a war.

They followed Andy Jackson to the Tallapoosa River where the Creek Indians were encamped behind timber fortifications waiting for the volunteers to arrive. Jackson would not disappoint and the fight would soon begin.

The night before the attack, the men sat quietly without warming fires, with their bellies aching for food. Eli struck up a whispering conversation with a young Major. Eli reached out his hand and said, "I'm Eli MacGowan, from McMinn County, Tennessee, these are my sons", as he pointed to and named each.

The young Major said, "I'm Sam Houston from Blount County, Tennessee." Eli and Sam exchanged some chat, about missing the mountains, their families back home and the like. Passing the night away, not being able to sleep.

Morning came to Eli and so did his orders. They were to make a frontal assault on the fortifications with the regular army. Eli prayed with and for his men, including three of his sons, knowing they would face death in some form today. He felt mixed emotions, fear for his sons, his men, and an equal feeling of pride that they were willing to come and fight for a cause, even though Eli sometimes wondered if the cause was a just one.

Eli prayed for his men and after the prayer was over he said, "My sons and brothers, I ask only two things of you, first that you kill before you are killed and second that you know this *is* war and you will see and do things that you will question until the day you die, hopefully, as an old man. Do not question anything that happens here today, on this battlefield, just get through this alive, and we will all go back to our mountain homes in Tennessee, to our families and children. May God bless you all."

The Cherokees attacked the Creeks from the rear of the horseshoe, to draw them to the rear, away from the fortress wall fronting Eli's men. Jackson gave word to attack the barricade. The volunteers and regular army charged, screaming as loud as a human could. The screams of the same ferocity echoing still from every battlefield in Scotland.

Eli led them straight ahead and over the wall. He slashed with his bayonet, fired once and as many times as he chanced taking time to reload. He dodged hatchets and tomahawks. It was fierce, and bloody. Eli and his men killed many Creeks. They tried to save the women and children. Eli hoped his sons were not hacking and shooting women and children either.

The battle lasted for hours, and then it was eerily quiet.

Eli scanned the field for his sons. He was relieved, when his count added up the right number. He could see they all had that look on their faces. Eli remembered the same look on the faces of the young men on top of King's Mountain that morning, the morning his brother Isaac died.

Blood spattered their faces and their clothes. He saw their cut hands and arms bleeding from being hacked in defending their heads from hatchet blows. Death littered the fertile river bottomland, it would never bear crops again, Eli feared. It would always be a graveyard for the dead, lost on this day.

General Jackson rode in and pranced around on his white mount, wearing his clean uniform, looking heroic. Jackson made eye contact with Eli while he was resting on a stump. Eli nodded, as he puffed his pipe, Jackson tipped his gaudy looking hat to him. Eli thought Jackson was a great man but he had seen enough of his actions to be worried about his hateful heart.

Jackson ordered headcounts, living, wounded and dead. Eli allowed that Jackson needed a detail number for his reports to the President. The only orders Eli wanted were the ones sending him home because he knew the Creeks had no fight left in them.

They buried the dead and cared for the wounded. Eli offered a prayer of thanks, that his men were all alive and able to travel.

Finally, orders came that the war was over and the brigade would return to Tennessee, for mustering out of this volunteer army. Eli could still remember the emotions of the day.

The march home was quick, they passed through villages of their fellow Cherokee soldiers and took as much rations as they could spare for the half-starved army.

He saw the villages of the Chickamauga and thought how

things in life come full circle. The same Cherokees that had raided the Watauga Settlements of his youth were now providing food for him, his sons and the rest of his soldiers.

Eli could see his valley home, finally he, and his sons, stepped onto the porch of the cabin. Maggie opened the door and with a somber expression said, "Eli, once again you have come back to me alive from a war, this time, bringing my sons back too. God has answered my prayers." She hugged and kissed the haggard looking group and cried. It was a good time.

Maggie asked the boys to stay and eat, but they wanted to see their families, so she told them, "Go, I'll see you all tomorrow, when we will feast and celebrate life, my sons."

Eli and Maggie sat on their porch and watched their sons ride off to their homes. He turned to Maggie and softly said, "Maggie, I am happy to see you and to know our home will be safe until the next war comes along. I hope I'll not see another one. I know the next war will have to come to me, because I am just too old to chase it anymore."

Maggie sat in his lap, hugged him and cried she didn't like the way Eli talked and knew he had seen terrible things. She hugged him and said, "It will get better, with time, my sweet Eli, it will get better."

Eli felt the contents of the churn thickening; this caused his thoughts to return to his chore. The state of the contents in the churn meant his chore was about over. He lifted the top of the churn and confirmed his thoughts. He took the cream ladle, scooped the butter up, and poured the buttermilk into a separate bowl. He worked the butter in the bowl, poured cold water over it, continued to work the butter, and finally started washing the butter to remove the last remnants of buttermilk.

Eli remembered his Granny Gullie telling his sisters about this step; otherwise, it would spoil the butter. He was glad he had paid attention to these details.

Eli sprinkled some salt on the butter and worked it in as he patted and squeezed the air out forming rounded balls of butter. He covered the butterballs with cloth and placed them into the clay crock, and poured the buttermilk into another crock jug, plugged it and carried his evenings work to the springhouse, to stay cool.

He thought back on the war, he wondered how many good men would have to die, before this country settled down and learned to live in peace. He knew there were plenty of men willing to fight in this valley. The sons of patriots could still inspire their sons to take up arms, for any fight.

The glory of war, Eli thought, was hard to clear from the heads of the young men and boys. Eli thought how a new generation had their war. They could sit and tell the stories of glory and pass it on to their sons and grandsons. He had seen enough carnage and death for his life and hoped that his grandsons would hear the horror of war from his sons and not just the glory side.

He knew the Generals, who led the young men to die, for *their* glory; they went on to become heroes, governors, and presidents.

To the young men, it was just killing before someone killed you. Eli could still remember the smell of war. He could remember the blood and hear the prayers and cries of dying boys and men.

It was a hard thing to figure, he thought that wars had to happen; countries had to protect their lands and people. A hard thing to figure indeed, he guessed he would end this debate in his head; go to bed, he was not smart enough to figure it out and would let it rest for tonight.

"Well, another day of sunshine burnt," he said to Dawg, as he stepped into the cabin. A warm supper and a cold bed were waiting, and he was ready for both tonight. He hoped for a sleep free from the images of war, a good, peaceful rest indeed.

CHAPTER SIX
DEATH IN THE VALLEY

Rain pecking on the roof of the cabin greeted Eli and Dawg on this morning. The kind of rain that you wished would turn into snow. Cold and steady, just enough to get a man soaked to the bone, a real chiller for sure.

Eli worked in the summer and spring rains, but these cold winter rains had become too much for his aging joints. He was resolved to stay in the dry today.

He was glad he had churned the night before, and his mouth was watering for some hot biscuits and fresh butter.

After finishing his breakfast, Eli and Dawg sloshed down to the barn to milk and feed. Once completed, he thought about the chestnut wood he had brought down for chair parts. "Yep Dawg, a good day for makin' chairs," he said.

Eli picked out the perfect pieces of chestnut limbs, shaved the bark and started shaping the parts. He often thought the chestnut was the perfect tree. The tree grew to one hundred feet if left alone, fifty feet to the first limbs and six feet across. It gave shade from the summer sun, nuts for roasting in the fall, and when cut it was the best timber for building. The wood was good for burning in the stove. Yep, he thought, the perfect tree, indeed.

Eli had some prime sections of white oak soaking for caning the chair bottoms. He retrieved these pieces and started the tedious work of making the long thin shavings for the chair bottoms.

Sitting on the workbench that his grandfather Angus had built, he quietly did his work. He pulled the two-handled shaper with the grain, each sliver of oak caning as near perfect as the previous one.

Once he had enough to cover the bottom of one chair, he started weaving the wet pliable oak caning to form the seat of his chairs. This work took strong hands, Eli MacGowan had what most men referred to as "paws", and he was proud of that achievement. His fingers were big enough to make two of most men's.

He learned the art of chair making and caning from his father; the MacGowans prided themselves on being crafty. It was not really being crafty but a skill for survival, a way to provide for their families and to make a living.

Eli remembered with a smile, trying to teach young Angus or Gussie, as they called him, his last-born son, this very art. It was not lack of effort on Gussie's part but lack of skill that created the wobbly splintered contraption that he proudly presented to his mother, on that Christmas Eve.

Maggie accepted the gift with her usual wide-eyed awe, she hugged the lad to the point that Eli thought his son would suffocate. *That* was Maggie and *that* was Gussie. They were without a doubt two of the kindest souls he had ever known.

The little bench was set in a corner of the cabin so that Maggie could admire her young son's handiwork every day as she did her chores in the cabin. Eli would often catch her smiling as she glanced at the "work of art." Eli had noticed the chair was missing from the cabin, he guessed Maggie had taken it with her to Calhoun. That was certainly fine with him, no reminders needed he thought.

Young Gussie was under foot all the time. He was always curious, asking questions without stopping to listen for the answers. He was the pride of his father and went with Eli every step he made.

Gussie was always the student; he loved going to school with his older sisters, Mattie and Gwen. The three of them dominated the settlement school, or so Mr. Shanks the schoolmaster, told Eli and Maggie.

The three youngest MacGowans could cipher, read, and write. Eli often wished his older children could have had access to such higher education. All they had was what Maggie could teach, which was considerable.

Eli could read, write, and do numbers but had no patience for teaching. His constitution would not allow him to be in one place that long. Maggie did an admirable job, and even found time to teach some of the neighboring families, before they built the settlement school.

Young Gussie, at age five could read with his sisters who were two and three years older. Eli thought they were exceptional and beamed with pride in their presence. Maybe he was too proud, thought Eli.

The day he first heard of the fever, in the settlement, never left Eli's memory. Maggie had wanted to send Gussie, Mattie, and Gwen to Calhoun, to stay with their son, Isaac; thinking getting away would keep them safe. Eli was too stubborn to allow that. He thought by keeping the children away from the settlement they would be safe.

It was a few summers ago when the Yellow Fever entered the settlement, in the blood of a new English immigrant settler. He was sick, as was his wife and two children; they lingered for a while but succumbed to the mysterious ailment.

That summer was hot and wet; little did Eli and Maggie know that these were deadly ingredients. The mosquitoes, which swarmed near the settlement, drew the blood from the sick immigrants, who had innocently carried this death to the valley.

The death angel visited many households that summer, taking one here and two there. Eli and Maggie MacGowan gave three.

A dark cloud came over the MacGowan cabin that summer. Maggie, Eli's mother, and the older son's wives tended to the sick children. Mattie was the first to fall ill; the fever was the start, then her young body started to bleed from every orifice, then she became quiet. They prayed and hoped she was sleeping. Sleeping to **death**, she was. From start to finish, this torture lasted the better part of two weeks. Gwen started showing signs after a few days, then Gussie.

In near panic, Maggie and Eli watched as one by one, their three youngest children became casualties of this unseen devil. Maggie's effort to save the children was in vain. She could do nothing but pray and keep cool cloths on their heads, she keep her fear inside, as did Eli's mother.

Eli and Maggie's daughters-in-law went back to their husbands in the settlement, when it was clear of the outcome. They had children to care for too and had crops to help harvest.

Eli prayed and made promises with God, he prayed aloud, "let them live and I'll be a better man," although all that knew him, considered him a fine man. He was an elder in the church, first to lend a hand in hard times, generous, and compassionate.

That was about to change.

Eli laid Mattie in the ground on a Tuesday, Gwen on Thursday and Gussie on Saturday. It rained hard when Eli laid young Gussie into the ground. That suited Eli fine, the rain hid his tears and the thunder concealed his furious shouts and cursing, at God.

Eli used his carpentry skills to build things he never expected to build. He chiseled the names of his children onto headstones to mark their graves. He built coffins, large and small, for his dead and the dead in the settlement.

After the death of his children, Eli disappeared for over a month. He went high into the mountains. He stood on the highest point of MacGowan Mountain, screamed, and cursed God. He said things that most men would be to fearful to think, much less say. Eli didn't care what God thought. He stood in the lightning and dared The Almighty to strike him dead, but He would not comply.

Eli grew weary and went home one early fall morning. Maggie and his mother were there, they looked pale and weak. They looked as if they had aged a decade that summer. They didn't speak much; Maggie stood at the one solitary window and looked at the little graves down the road. She cried often, as did Eli's mother, they could function *somehow*. They still cooked and did the chores.

Maggie and his mother often attempted to hug Eli but he would withdraw. They didn't press.

Night was a quiet time, except for the sobbing. Eli often heard his mother and Maggie crying until asleep. Eli didn't sleep much he just worked. Eli worked hard to keep from thinking. This worked, *most* of the time.

The time passed slowly and the fever left the land that winter, as it had arrived, quietly.

Eli thought the worst was finally over. Then one day he found his mother's cold body sitting on the porch. She had her eyes locked open, as if gazing on the graves of her dear grandchildren.

Eli could not bear for his mother to see that sad sight any longer and with his huge rough fingers, he gently closed her blue eyes, for the last time.

He carried her into the warm cabin and laid her frail, little body on the table. Maggie reached for Eli; he just turned and went to the barn to build yet another coffin.

He built his mother's coffin and headstone. He dug her grave beside her precious Mattie, Gwen, and young Gussie.

He carried the coffin to the table, where Maggie had prepared his mother's body. He helped Maggie lift his mother's lifeless body into the coffin and watched her comb her white hair for her wake.

The wake was a solemn affair as the visitors were all too grief stricken, from their recent losses, to grieve this night.

The Settlement Presbyterian Church had the funeral and most of the settlement attended. This little log church had seen this ritual performed too many times this year and looked sad and dark. It was the same sad and dark mood of the throng in its interior today.

Pastor Emmons said his now well-known burial sermon. He talked of the fine quality of woman that was William MacGowan's wife and Eli's mother. The service didn't melt Eli's icy heart; he endured the muttering words of Pastor Emmons, purely out of respect for his dead mother.

They carried and placed her into the open ground that Eli had prepared. Eli and Maggie's sons lowered her into her cold bed. They all consoled each other; Eli didn't desire consoling and left for the mountaintop once again. Eli cursed God even more vehemently, after his mother died.

He left Maggie alone with her grief, her sons and daughters were nearby, but she was still alone, without Eli.

Maggie spent most of the day sitting on Gussie's little bench that she had placed near his grave. She planted flowers on all the graves in the spring and tended to them daily, watering them during the dry days of early summer.

Eli visited the cabin about once a month for the next six months. He would stay to himself for a day or two and disappear again. Dawg would try to follow, but he would send him back to Maggie.

Maggie was lost; being without a child to care for was an adjustment that she was unprepared to cope with, at this time in her life. She began to wither away, just as the apple, when not harvested from the tree, dries up when it not used for its intended purpose.

More time passed, Eli made no offer to make peace with the All Mighty and he became hateful towards Maggie. She *still* tried to console him but he was granite in his feelings and her tender pleading could not open his heart. Maggie could not bear to see Eli this way, so she left.

The flowers Maggie planted withered and died.

A clap of thunder jarred Eli; he was back on task making the chairs. His heart was full of emotions. Too full, he thought to think about. He continued to work on the chairs and hoped for no more thinking about his loss.

Eli shaved the parts for the frame of another chair, until they were smooth. He drilled the holes, with his brace and bit, and tapped the parts into place. He finished one frame and started on another. This continued until he completed and assembled six chairs.

He stood back and admired his work of the day. This day had melted away he needed to milk and feed. His belly was complaining at its empty state but his belly would have to wait until the chores were completed.

Eli worked well unto the evening and completed the rest of his chores and slowly walked up the hollow to the dark cabin, ate his supper and again crawled into the cold bed.

Eli's last thoughts were of Maggie as he drifted off to sleep.

CHAPTER SEVEN
SWEET MAGGIE

Down the Hiwassee River at her son Isaac's place in Calhoun, a half days ride from Eli MacGowan, lay Maggie in her feather bed. Maggie was having a hard time finding sleep this night. She had said her prayers, putting in a special word for Eli, as usual, continuing through the entire MacGowan family. Her heart was especially heavy tonight wondering how Eli was faring.

She was a sweet soul indeed, a saintly woman most would say. She stood tall and straight. She was a loving mother, wife and grandmother. Her heart was broken and she was not complete without Elijah MacGowan. They were truly one flesh. She grieved for him almost as if he was in the ground with her darling children.

She rolled to her side and viewed the moon as it glittered off the ripples of the river. Her second story room allowed for a view of the valley, she scanned upward and saw the moon as it peaked from behind MacGowan Mountain in the distant valley. She thought how Eli was in his bed by now with Dawg resting on the porch. A tear trickled onto her pillow and she said one last prayer for Eli and drifted off to sleep.

She dreamed of her mother and father sitting on the porch in Bent Mountain in the Virginia hills. They watched Maggie and her brothers and sisters as they played under the old oaks that shaded the little cabin.

Her flaming red hair flowed down her back from under the little bonnet that capped her head. She could see her brothers playing tag and racing around the cabin, hiding behind the trees. Laughter filled the Johnson Hollow and echoed down the valley to her uncles and grandparents cabins nearby. She could hear her mother calling the children to wash up for supper. Maggie hated this time of day, but complied with her mother's orders.

"Let us pray" her father said, they all joined hands and listened as their father spoke reverently in a soft deep Scottish voice. His words were direct and to the point, simply "Our heavenly father, bless this food for our bodies, thank you for your bounty and the person who has prepared this meal, may it nourish our bodies. Amen."

Maggie remembered standing at the side of the table, since there were not enough chairs to go around, and the benches were already full of Johnson children. She thought how they always had plenty of food to eat, since they labored hard and had good land. A blessed family she thought.

She loved their place on the mountain and remembered the day her father and mother announced that they would be moving to Watauga. Maggie and most of the younger children looked puzzled not knowing where this strange sounding land was. There were no questions; the words of her father and mother had settled this.

In the following weeks, the cabin contents were loaded into the wagons. Maggie's oldest brother John inherited some of the items of his father and mother. He was married and had two young sons. Maggie's grandmother would stay with John until the following spring after they had settled in a bit.

Maggie was heartbroken at the prospect of leaving her brother and young nephews behind. She wondered if she would see them again, being so far away.

Maggie watched John, his wife and two young sons as they faded from view of the wagons as they rattled down the path towards Watauga. Maggie's sadness soon turned into excitement as they left the valley for the first time in her life. They spent the nights in churchyards they passed along the way, feeling secure in a certain protection the All Mighty would provide.

They journeyed past cabins and fields of spring corn just sprouting. She remembered her father bemoaning the fact that his crops would be late this year, but he didn't worry, he had faith that their needs would be provided. Maggie thought that they always had been.

They played games as they rode along the journey, slept under the open stars, cooked over an open fire each night. They washed in streams, drank the cool mountain water, and just enjoyed the company of each other.

The journey provided meetinghouses for worship, brush arbors were sometime the only churches available. Maggie loved church meetings, she would sing the hymns her mother and father had taught them from earliest memory. "Bringing in the Sheaves" was her favorite.

The day finally came, her mother said, "youngins we will be on our new land by nightfall." Those words were welcome and sad at the same time. Maggie knew their happy times they had enjoyed would be over. It would also spell the start of the hard spring work to get the cabin in order and crops in the ground.

Maggie could still remember the words of her father as he introduced himself to William MacGowan. She remembered the commotion of the Johnson clan as they evacuated the wagon that day.

She opened the flap and there was a fine strapping young man that looked at her as none had looked at her before. That was her first glimpse of Elijah MacGowan, who unbeknownst to her would be her mate for life. She took the gourd water dipper he offered and drank it up. Eli just stared at her with that big toothy grin that had become so familiar to her.

From that day they were inseparable, mates for life.

CHAPTER EIGHT
JACK MANKILLER

The morning came and Eli could tell from the brightness in the cabin that it had snowed during the night. He looked out the door and saw a blanket of snow laying down the hollow. He thought today would be a good day to set his traps.

After breakfast, Eli grabbed some fat meat and placed it in a sack, slung it over his shoulder, and headed to the barn. He grabbed a dozen steel traps and headed down MacGowan Creek.

About three miles or so out, he set his first trap. He placed the fat meat for bait, tapped the anchor into the hard ground below the water, opened the trap jaws, and gingerly set it below the cold water.

Eli liked to set his traps so the minks, muskrats, or beavers would drown once the critter sprung the trap. This was the way his father had taught him, drowning was much better than letting the animal gnaw its leg trying to get free from the trap.

He spent most of the cold winter day crunching along the creek bank, setting the traps. He was finishing the last trap when he looked up and saw a figure standing beside his horse, across the creek.

He was a lanky looking man, covered head to foot with a hooded buckskin robe holding the reigns to a Red Roan horse. Eli could not see his face because the shadow cast by the robe concealed it. He could see the leather breeches and moccasins so he allowed that it must be an Indian.

Eli stood up straight and shook the creek water from his cold reddened hands. The twenty feet of creek separating the two, was not very comforting to Eli. He had not brought his gun today and he could see a partially exposed rifle peeking out from the sheath on the stranger's saddle.

Neither spoke right off, then the stranger said, "got any corn pone and coffee you old Scot?" Instantly a grin curled across Eli's leathery face and he felt at ease. He knew the voice, as well as any he had ever heard, and as the Indian removed the robe from his head, his old eyes confirmed what his ears had suspected.

There stood Jack Mankiller. It *was* Jack all right, but an older version of the man Eli had known for over sixty years. Jack grinned, revealing the spaces where he once had teeth. Eli chuckled and spoke "looks like you and your teeth have had a bit of a fallin' out."

Jack replied, with a grin, "I can still call you Gigage Gitlu (gee ga gay gee tloo) even if you have white hair now." Eli thought how long it had been since anyone had called him Gigage Gitlu or Red Hair. Eli laughed and replied "true, my friend, maybe you will call me Yonega Gitlu (yo na gah gee tloo) or White Hair?"

"No," said Jack, "you will *always* be Red Hair," as he mounted his horse and crossed MacGowan Creek to join Eli. Jack dismounted and they embraced and backed up a pace and looked at each other.

They gazed and smiled, sizing each other up, Eli slapped Jack on the back and made the dust fly from the musty old robes that sheltered the old Cherokee's bones.

"Did you lose your straight razor," asked Jack? He said, "You used to be so fond of it," as he tugged on the base of Eli's foot long white beard. Eli smiled; he had not shaved nor cut his hair, since days of the fever.

Jack noticed a handmade splint that binding around Eli's forearm and inquired, "What have you done to your arm Eli?"

"Ah, I took a tumble off a bluff and cracked it a little; weren't no bone stickin' out so I reckon this splint will keep it 'til it mends back in a few weeks."

"Gettin' a little wobbly are you Eli, better be careful about that fallin'," he laughed.

Eli said, "come to the cabin and sit with me and we'll talk, it is too cold for old men to be out today." Jack said, "I could use a good warm fire."

They both walked their horses back up the creek. And Jack made quick friends with Dawg on the journey. "What is the mutt's name?" inquired Jack. Eli replied "Dawg," Jack chuckled and thought, yes that is Eli MacGowan, thrifty with everything, even words.

"Why *would* you want to waste words namin' a dog?" said Jack. He laughed and patted Dawg on his old head.

Once at the cabin, Eli stoked the fire and both men pulled off their wet boots to roast their toes by the stove. Eli filled two pipes and handed one to Jack, they fired both up and puffed the room nearly full of smoke before they spoke.

Mankiller spoke first, "Eli, I stopped at Isaac's place yesterday and spent the night." Eli didn't acknowledge the commentary; he just looked up and watched a circle of smoke, from his pipe, as it rose to the ceiling. Jack continued to speak, "Isaac and his family are doing well, and he *is* a MacGowan, through and through, he's got *eleven* youngins!" Eli grinned, but tried to conceal it from Jack.

Eli said, "He had ten youngins' the last time I saw him." Jack said "they are a good lookin' brood Eli; you should get down to Calhoun, and see them." Again, Eli had no response. Jack thought he would let it be for now.

Eli, changing the subject, said "what have we become Jack?" "We were once young and life was easy for us, all we had to worry about was our next meal." Jack grunted and nodded his agreement.

Eli said, "Speakin' of our next meal, Jack, I'm hungry!" Eli rose and started supper; Jack went to the smokehouse and fetched some sizable slabs of ham. Eli prepared a feast that night, at least to his standards it was. He fixed ham, biscuits, gravy, butter, molasses, and coffee. They both gorged on the victuals that had festooned their tin plates and cups, until they were stuffed.

Eli went to the springhouse and drew a bucket of water, put it in a pan on the stove, once heated he placed the supper plates in to soak. He thought they would keep until morning to wash. He had company and needed to mind his manners and chat.

Jack and Eli propped their chairs on two legs, and leaned it against the cabin wall. They lit the pipes and started talking again. Neither Jack nor Eli was big talkers and both could be quiet for long periods, without being uncomfortable.

Jack started the conversation, "I remember the first time I saw your old red head. My father was in Watauga, sellin' backer and you were with your father in the tradin' post. We sat on the porch; you gave me a piece of candy and told me your name was Eli MacGowan."

Jack said, "I guess we were seven or eight, I ate the candy, it was horehound, and it was good." Eli replied, "I think we were seven. You gave me a bear you had carved and I said I could not take it, you said yes, for the candy."

Eli got up and walked over to the mantle, picked up an object and handed it to Jack. It was the little carved bear from over sixty years ago. Eli said, "It is one of my most cherished things, I look at it and it brings a smile to my face when nothing else will. This little bear has kept me company, so many dark nights, my brother."

Jack rubbed his thumb over the little bear and a tear ran down his face. Eli saw the tear and blinked his eyes to stop an equal response. There had been many hard days since the little boys exchanged gifts that day so many years ago. These men of seventy with worn joints, failing teeth, and long white hair, were seven again. Their hearts raced and the wind whistled through their ears. They were young and back in the Watauga Valley. Their friendship began on that summer day at the trading post; it was the foundation of their friendship of six decades.

Eli and Jack ran and played with the MacGowan, Johnson, and Mankiller children but Eli and Jack were like brothers.   The main thing they had in common was a love for exploring, which they did every chance they had. These two intimately knew every mountain and valley that was within a day's walk of Watauga. They knew every game trail, every path, ridge and stream. They knew where the best berries were in the summer and where the best chestnuts and walnuts were in the fall.

Jack would often help Eli with his chores so he could have more exploration time. The MacGowans gradually looked at Jack as one of the family. He would eat at their table and sleep at their cabin.

When it was time to go home, Jack's sister Betty would come to retrieve him. Betty Mankiller was a beauty and would eventually become Eli's brother James' wife. This arrangement only allowed

Jack more time around the MacGowan place, since James and Betty built their cabin only a half mile away.

Eli would go with the Cherokees on hunts; it was an honor for Eli, since hunting was one of the most important duties that Cherokee men had. Eli savored the time spent with the Cherokee; they welcomed another hunter, especially one as good as Eli.

He always gave his kills to his hosts, because the MacGowans always had more than enough to get through the winters. This act of generosity only endeared him more to the Cherokees.

The Cherokees honored Eli and called him Gigage Gitlu or Red Hair. The Cherokees in their usual simplistic manner just called him Red.

The Cherokee people loved life, although sometimes life was harsh. They, like the Scots, overcame, adapted, and persevered. Eli loved the Cherokee people; it was a sentiment *not* shared by all of the settlers, especially the newcomers.

The newcomers envied the Cherokee farms. The Cherokee farms occupied some of the best bottomland and long before the Scots and others arrived, were very productive farms. Eli and Jack felt the rumblings in the valley and knew the years of peace could be ending. It saddened Eli to think that the pressure for land had reasonable people talking about moving the Cherokees off their land.

When he tried to discuss this with Jack, he just smiled and said, "The Cherokees ran Indians off this land and took it, so I expect the same will happen to us someday." Eli pondered a minute or two on that one and said, "Dern Jack, maybe you ought to be in politics." They both laughed.

The two old friends continued to reminisce into the night. Eli said, "My eyes are heavy." Jack laughed and said, "We need to turn in, we are too old to stay up, it is near two hours after sunset." They both chuckled and hit the tick for the night.

"Eli," said Jack, "Maybe we can figure out all the problems of this world tomorrow, or maybe just start with the ones in this cabin tonight."

Eli looked through the open door where Jack lay in bed, looking at Eli and said, "Maybe someone should mind their pints and quarts."

Jack laughed and Eli blew out the lamp and rolled over for a good rest.

He tossed around in the shuck bed with thoughts of Maggie grating in his head. He knew Jack was here to soften him up, "Dern it," Eli growled under his breath. He and Jack would talk more in the morning.

CHAPTER NINE
DRAGGING CANOE COMES TO THE VALLEY

The sweet scent of ham frying filled Eli's nostrils. Was he dreaming? Nope! He opened his eyes to the sight of Jack Mankiller cooking breakfast.

"Thought me rattlin' around would do the trick," said Jack. Eli rubbed his eyes and sat on the edge of the bed. He slid into his breeches and took in a deep breath.

"It's been a long while since I have slept through the night," said Eli as he walked through the cabin door to relieve his bladder from the porch.

Dawg was up and waiting on the porch. Eli had left him out all night and Dawg had a look that didn't show too much appreciation over the matter. Eli said "well, Dawg; looks like you ain't froze to death."

Dawg grunted his distain, stretched, and yawned. "We might have a scrap or two for you later if you can stay awake," said Eli. Dawg didn't acknowledge Eli's comments but walked down the steps hiked his leg and marked his territory on Eli's whittlin' bench. Eli only chuckled at Dawg's statement and went back into the cabin.

Jack was busy stirring the gravy; he was a much better cook than Eli was; although Eli's skills were getting better since Maggie's departure. Jack had lived most of his life without a steady woman. Jack said, "Set down my brother. I have made good use of your food stores." "It sure looks good," said Eli.

Jack slid the eggs onto Eli's plate. Biscuits and ham soon joined the eggs. Jack then poured the gravy over the plate and sat down to join Eli.

They ate like starved wolves, clanking and scraping the forks on the tin plates. They slurped down two cups of strong coffee. Lastly, they put two biscuits on the plate, put a dollop of butter on each and covered them with blackstrap molasses.

"Whew" said Eli, "I have not had a meal like that since Maggie left." Since Eli mentioned her name, Jack took the opportunity to speak about Maggie.

"Eli, my brother, I talked to Maggie at Isaac's place. She misses you Red." Eli didn't reply, but he heard Jack's words and that was all Jack wanted for now. With Eli MacGowan, Jack knew that there was a time to talk, and a time for not talking. Now was a time for **not** talking.

"Well, Jack let me clean up the plates and we'll go check my traps." Jack nodded and filled his pipe to wait on Eli to finish his domestic chores.

They covered up for the cold and headed for the creek. The snow had a hard crust because of the cold of the night.

There was a method to trap checking. Eli would go to the end of the trap sets and work back towards the cabin. That way you carried your animals back and not down and back. At least that was the way Eli had it figured.

They said nothing, as they walked to the end of the sets on MacGowan Creek, back up the last trap. Each man knew what needed doing. There was not much need for chatting. Eli observed that critters had sprung five of the twelve traps and were occupying a cold watery grave. Two minks and three muskrats, he counted as they baited and reset each trap. They walked back to the barn and Eli retrieved the pelt stretchers, as Jack was busy skinning the stiff critters.

Once skinned, they each started scraping the pelts. They carefully stretched the pelts and tacked them beside their critter cousins already on the barn wall. He was a bit behind on his trapping this winter. Eli thought, but didn't say, because of doing Maggie's work.

Jack and Eli admired the mornings work, washed up in the cold creek water, and sat on the bench for a rest. They fired up the pipes and puffed. Eli chuckled and looked at Jack. Eli said, "Do you remember trapping on the Watauga River when we were youngins'?"

Jack chuckled. "I remember the time we ran up on that barr eatin' a mushrat, we had in the trap. You thought you'd run it off, but the barr thought otherwise." Eli laughed out loud and said, "what a day to leave the guns at the cabin."

Jack remembered, "I beat that barr off you a while and you beat 'em off me." Eli said, "We must have beat on that barr for the best part of an hour, 'til he give up the ghost!" "We still have the scars," said Jack, as he and Eli traced the remnants of the teeth marks on their hands.

That was where the legend of Jack and Red began, with the Cherokees. What a site the fourteen year olds were, as they walked into the Cherokee settlement, with the gutted two hundred pound black bear, tied to a carrying pole. They were both bloody and exhausted from the fight and the trip. The toothy grin they both had plastered on their bloody faces would be unforgettable, by anyone lucky enough to witness the site.

Word spread to the white settlements too, and soon a crowd gathered to witness the sight and listen to the tales the two lads had to tell. They were not short on details, as they relayed the tale to the gathered throng. The eyes were wide open on the younger children, Cherokees and settlers alike. Even the elders were enthralled and in admiration of the accomplishment of this pair.

From that day on, Eli and Jack's fathers looked with pride at their youngest sons. It didn't go without notice on the young females either, once word of their bear killing prowess spread.

Maggie now looked at Eli with awe; she knew at fourteen, that he would be her man, if he would have her. Eli thought about marriage, but figured he would at least wait until he was sixteen, just to be sure.

Jack took advantage of his new fame and made solid acquaintance with a few of the pretty Cherokees and near Cherokees.

Several of the early Scot and French trappers had taken Cherokee wives. Their daughters were beauties and ranged from dark skinned to near white, some even with red hair. Jack Mankiller's first love was one of these near Cherokee girls.

Her name was Becky Walker and she lived as a Cherokee, but looked as Scottish as Eli. Jack, Becky, Eli, and Maggie were together as much as old married couples, except for the times when Jack and Eli would break away, to explore or hunt.

Eli and Jack were up on the Doe River hunting and exploring for a few weeks when unbeknownst to them, trouble was brewing in the Watauga Valley. The problem was some of the Cherokees down south, were angry over the sale of the lands to the whites.

One of these, Dragging Canoe of the Chickamaugas had decided to stir up trouble. He went on a killing rampage, burning cabins and killing settlers. Had it not been for Nancy Ward, Dragging Canoe's cousin and a Cherokee war-woman, sending word to the Watauga Valley s settlers, they would have certainly died.

They managed to fight off the Cherokees and quickly settled the situation with the help of Colonel Sevier and the militia. Although the battle was short lived, Becky Walker had the misfortune to be working in the fields, on the day when Dragging Canoe and followers came through.

Becky's father was off, with the militia, fighting and Becky was tending to the corn and to her younger brothers that day. She heard the screams of her mother and saw her run from the barn. She froze in horror, as the ball from a long rifle struck a deathblow in her mother's back and Becky watched, as she crumpled onto the plowed field.

Becky grabbed her siblings and headed toward the neighbors, but a ball struck her down in the same manner as her mother. She lay in the plowed furrows of her father's field, as life flowed from her fourteen-year-old body. Her young brothers pulled and begged her to rise, she said "run, **run!** as fast as you can."

She watched her eight-year-old brother plead with his two younger brothers to run, as he stayed to protect his fallen sister. He stood, like a little warrior, and fought. His only weapons were the hard clods of dirt from the plowed field that he threw at the oncoming raiders.

As her eyes dimmed she saw a knife cut her young brother's head almost off at the shoulders, he stood for an instance then fell. Becky gurgled, on her own blood, as she prayed.

Her young beautiful life was over.

While Eli and Jack were heading back home from their hunting and trapping trip, they visited the post at Roan Mountain. They heard the news about the Dragging Canoe raiders. They could not believe they had missed the fight. They sold their pelts and headed back down the Doe River, as fast as they could.

They had all sorts of images and questions filling their heads. Eli said, "Jack I'm a feared for our folks, what if they are killed?" Jack said, "What about Maggie and Becky?" They walked and ran, without talking again. They each knew what the other was thinking. Not knowing, was *not* good.

Eli and Jack arrived at the Mankiller's place first. Jack's folks looked at Eli in a strange manner. Jack's father had a worried look and said "Eli stay outside on the porch, I need to tell Jack something in private." Eli thought this strange; he had *always* been welcome, in the Mankiller's cabin.

The wait was uncomfortably long, to Eli. Jack walked out, he didn't say a word, and he just kept walking. Eli followed him; they headed towards the Walker's Place. Eli asked Jack, "why ain't you talkin', my brother?" Jack didn't reply, only kept walking towards Becky's cabin.

Before reaching the Walker's cabin, Eli saw new graves; he counted each, seven in all. As he drew closer, he started reading the names on the wooden headstones. There on the end, it stood, a rough sawn oak board with the simple letters carved to form two words, Becky Walker.

Jack melted onto the grave. He wrapped his arms around the oak grave marker as though he was holding Becky. Eli stood and witnessed the sight, not knowing what to do with himself. Jack lay on the fresh grave as darkness came. Eli sat with his back to a hickory tree and cried with Jack. They didn't speak through the night.

Eli wondered about his family and Maggie but he thought he didn't really want to know. Jack needed him right now and he would stay with his Cherokee brother.

Morning came, Jack nudged Eli on the knee and said, "Let's go Eli." Jack headed towards the Walker cabin, as they walked by the barn they could see inside the dark structure. They caught a glimpse of sight they would never forget. Hanging from the barn rafters was Tom Walker, Becky's father. Propped nearby was the shovel he had used to bury his wife and children.

They gazed, in horror, as they tried figured out what to do. Eli said, "Hold Tom's feet and push him up while I cut the rope loose." Eli felt the rope go limp and he cut it loose from the barn post. Instantly Tom's weight was on Jack and Eli quickly grabbed his head before it struck the barn floor.

This was the first time either of the young boys had touched a dead man. It was something neither would ever forget. They put Tom Walker's body in the handcart, and covered him with a blanket. They wheeled him out to the new cemetery he had recently established. They dug a grave and laid the blanket down and placed Tom in its midst. Mr. Walker looked stiff and blue, but peaceful somehow. They said nothing, but covered his body, pounded in a board and carved Tom Walker crudely on the top.

Both boys stood back and took in the sight; it was almost more than one could comprehend. Eli wondered if the same fate lay ahead of him at the MacGowan Farm.

"I guess we should say some words," Eli said. Jack said, "You say what you want and I'll listen but the dead can't hear." Eli tried to remember the words of scripture but nothing would come to him. He just said "Amen."

They didn't bother returning the cart, or the shovel; they started walking towards the MacGowans. Conversation was thin on the hour-long trek. Eli and Jack had no time for speaking; their heads were full of images that would keep them awake for weeks to come.

Eli's heart leapt when he saw his younger sisters running to greet him they grabbed Eli and Jack, hugged them, and cried. "We thought you were dead," said Annie. Eli heard his mother screaming as she ran towards him.

He ran and joined her. She hugged and kissed her son. "We thought you two were dead for sure," as Jack walked within her reach, she latched onto him, hugged, and kissed him in the same manner as Eli. She took each by the hand and they walked to the cabin.

William MacGowan sat on the porch, looking haggard and worn. He weakly stood and hugged his son and Jack.

Eli's mother said through her tears, "you boys look starved, I am fixin' for your father, sit and it will soon be ready."

Eli, Jack and William sat, without speaking, with worn and weary expressions. William put his arm around the boys and told of the defense of the valley and how fierce Dragging Canoe had fought and how many good men, of the settlement, had been hacked, or shot to death. It would take a long time to heal the wounds.

Eli told his father of the Walkers. William said, "the Walkers were fine people, Tom Walker fought by my side this week, it's just not right."

He wept openly; it was the first time Eli had seen his father cry. They all three cried there on the MacGowan porch, on that beautiful morning, they were broken, but they were alive.

It was a hard time.

The treatment of most Cherokees was different after the Dragging Canoe Raids, Eli and Jack didn't care, nor did the MacGowans; the Mankillers would always be welcome, at the MacGowan place.

Jack Mankiller never found anyone he could love like Becky Walker. He had women through the years, they were mere companions for a while, never anyone he would or could love.

So this was the hand they had been dealt. Jack lost his Becky to the Dragging Canoe Raiders and Eli had run his love off to his son's place.

CHAPTER TEN
LET'S GO HUNTIN'

Eli and Jack sat puffing their pipes in the barn with the smell of muskrat and mink pelts mingled with the cow and horse manure. They were just two old coots without a good woman. How pathetic they were, they probably deserved each other.

Eli slapped Jack on the knee and said "ain't we pretty dern pitiful Jack. Let's quit sittin' here talkin' old times. Let's go huntin'!"

They stood and felt their joints snap into place and went to the cabin and fetched their rifles and a ham chunk and biscuit.

Dawg looked cozy on the porch but Eli ordered him to work. "Let's go Dawg as he handed him a chunk of ham. Time to earn your keep; we've got a cravin' for some fresh meat for supper."

Dawg complained, with a growl; after all, it *was* cold and snowy. He probably thought these old men were starting to go daft for wanting to crunch around in the mountains today, but he slowly stretched up and joined them.

Off they went, hoping to pass the afternoon away with a little hunting and exploration. They headed up MacGowan Creek to where it forked into Spring Creek and walked the three miles of this clear cascading stream, to its source, the Blue Spring.

The azure blue spring gracefully rolled from under a sandstone ledge that protruded from a near vertical rock bluff. This was the namesake for the creek. Eli had never measured the depth of the spring, but he reckoned that it must be fifty feet deep. It just went out of site, turning to black. This was one of his favorite places on his land.

Eli often sat and studied things here. The sandstone bluffs that surrounded the spring often reminded Eli of how the grand cathedrals of Edinburgh must have looked. Granny Gullie talked of the one she and Angus had seen once when departing her beloved Scotland.

This place was sacred to the Cherokee and Eli allowed them to use it freely. Sometimes, late at night in the summer, he would see the distant lights of hunting fires and hear the Cherokees chanting.

He could certainly understand why they felt the reverence to this place. Eli had often come here to pray and read The Bible, back before he started his grudge, with the All Mighty.

Eli turned and saw that Jack had started a warming fire in the old charcoaled rock pit, near the spring. He parked his tail on the log to join him. Dawg made himself at home at Jack's feet.

They broke out the pipes, loaded up and started puffing. Eli reached into his coat pocket, retrieved a corked bottle, and handed it to Jack. "Here warm your bones from the inside." Jack uncorked the bottle, tipped it and felt the warmth of MacGowan's finest Scotch whisky spread down to his belly.

Jack took another sip and corked the bottle. He offered it back to Eli but he declined and said, "Stick it in your pocket." Jack chuckled and said, "I forgot, you make the best whisky in this part of the state but you *still* do not drink it." Eli replied, "I take a taste for medicine if I am feelin' poorly." They both grinned and looked down the valley.

The view from Blue Spring was well worth the walk. You could see the entire valley below. The snow of the previous night lay like a cotton blanket over the land. The skies had cleared to make way for a clear blue backdrop.

Eli had seen the little wisps of smoke increase through his time on MacGowan Mountain. It saddened him to see the outsiders moving into the valley across the Hiwassee River, even though he was an outsider at one time. He knew his beloved privacy would soon be gone with the increasing settlements.

He sat and thought how he had envisioned his sons and daughters living on their piece of his land grant. They wanted their own lands and he understood that feeling. Land was plentiful and more available as the government purchased more and more of the Cherokee lands.

Eli had watched his children move to lands, into North Georgia and throughout the Tennessee Valley. They were at most a two-day ride from him. He never made the journey to visit, anymore.

He thought they probably came to see Maggie, but didn't bother to travel the fifteen miles to see him. His hateful ways were to blame. He was content with the way things were, or at least that is what he had convinced himself to think lately.

Dawg sprang to life his head high in the air. He measured the scent passing through his broad head. Turning left, then right, he marked his course and took off, like a ball fired from Eli's long rifle.

Jack said, "Time to go to huntin'." "I reckon so," said Eli. Standing up they knocked out their pipes, kicked some snow into the simmering warming fire, and headed toward Dawg's howling.

Eli said "lets follow the foot of the bluff around to Maggie's Branch, sounds like that's where Dawg is headed." Jack nodded his concurrence and they crunched their way through the snow toward Dawg's constant barking. They walked gingerly through the snow and over the ice covered rocks. They could hear Dawg; his familiar tracking yelp was hard to miss.

They were nearing Maggie's Branch, named for his Maggie. Eli named the stream, it was his land, and time would tell if the name would stick. He often thought how the names changed through the change of ownership. The Cherokees had surely changed the names from the previous occupiers they fought off this land. Most of the Cherokee names had stuck with the settlers. Hiwassee River, Conasauga Creek, Ocoee River, and Chilhowee Mountain, all were still keeping their Cherokee names.

He wondered if his mountain went by another name before the settlement people started calling it MacGowan Mountain. He would have to ask Corntassel the next time he was at MacAndrews Mercantile, he thought.

He was getting close to Dawg and they saw the trail of what he was chasing. Jack and Eli's eyes widened as it registered on both of them, what Dawg was tracking. They had hoped it was a fat doe, but they knew without a doubt that the signs on the ground were not that of a doe but of feral hogs.

Eli was a good tracker, but there was never any doubt that Jack Mankiller was the best tracker in the valley. Jack turned to Eli and said, "I make it to be three or maybe four hogs," Eli nodded his agreement.

They knew that Dawg would be in trouble, being the only dog in the hunt. Pack hunting was the only safe way to hunt hogs and bears.

They picked up the pace. When younger, Eli and Jack could maintain a trot for hours, when tracking. After a few minutes, they stopped to listen for Dawg. The crunchy snow made it hard to hear while trotting. They needed to wait until their labored breathing settled down too.

They could hear Dawg and didn't like the sound. They took off again. They saw that Dawg had the hogs cornered against a rock bluff. Normally wild hogs would try to run, but they had no way to escape and Dawg intended to keep them cornered. One hog would nip at him and Dawg would nip back. Jack and Eli yelled, as they ran into the fray. The hogs hardly acknowledged the human entry into this life and death drama.

Eli could see that Dawg was emboldened by their appearance and lurched towards the largest of the hogs. He was a massive boar, twice Dawg's size, with wicked curled tusks measuring half a foot long. With his course hair standing high on his back, he wielded his tusks like sabers, intent on killing Dawg. As Dawg lurched, the boar's running mates scattered and headed towards Jack and Eli. In unison, Eli and Jack, raised their rifles and fired, each striking a hog in the head. They stumbled and fell to their death, the count was whittled somewhat. The big boar was still slashing his way into Dawg's shaggy old sides.

Jack stopped to reload, as Eli continued towards the fight. He jumped on the back of one of the foul smelling critters and slashed his throat, with his long knife. Only the big boar remained, Eli and Dawg were in a bad spot. He could see Dawg's guts strung out of a long gash in his belly. The old boar got his licks in, but was about to pay the price, for his action.

Eli heard the crack of Jack's rifle and saw the old boar drop out of the fight. Jack's long rifle had splattered the forehead of the old boar onto the snow. The piercing, squealing, snorting, and barking, was now only a whimper.

Eli looked at Jack and nodded his thanks. Eli focused on his old bloody friend lying on the snow. Jack turned his attention to Dawg also. He was in bad shape. Eli had patched Dawg up many times throughout the years, but this was *bad*. Dawg tried to stand, Eli said, "stay still you old fool, you know better than to take on these hogs by yourself." Dawg knew Eli's scolding was only because he loved him, the old dog only weakly fell back, looked at Eli with sad, old eyes, and whimpered. Eli, only patted his old friend and felt a lump forming in his throat, he did not speak.

Jack sliced the throats of one of the hogs that was still showing signs of life, just to be sure. He didn't want his or Eli's entrails hanging out because of lack of attention to the hogs.

Jack walked over to where Dawg lay. Eli said "it's bad ain't it Jack." Jack trying to give Eli and Dawg some hope he said, "Seen worse, let's get him closed up."

Jack kicked the snow out to clear a spot and started a fire. Eli took off his coat and pulled off his shirt to use for bandages. They knew they had to be quick, and they moved as quickly as their cold joints would allow.

With the fire burning, Jack heated his knife and proceeded to sear closed as many bleeders as he could on the old dog. After looking for any remaining punctures, and finding none, Eli started to get busy placing Dawg's entrails back into his body. Dawg was out from the shock and blood loss, so Eli didn't worry about being too easy with the procedure. Time was Dawg's enemy.

Eli and Jack started stitching the gash in Dawg's abdomen closed. There were skills that could save your life and every backwoodsman learned early on how to close a wound. They always had a needle and some thread with them, just in case.

Jack and Eli washed off in Maggie's Branch and sat down for a minute to smoke and warm by the fire. They had placed Dawg on a bed of pine needles and he looked at peace, warm by the fire.

Eli watched Dawg's breathing, it was shallow and slow, he wondered aloud to Jack. "Will he make it Jack?" Jack just tilted his head to the side and puffed his pipe. He thought to himself that they might as well dig a hole and bury the old mutt, but he knew how much this dog meant to Eli, and only said, "We'll see."

Jack rose to his feet and said, "I'll go fetch the horse and we can tote him back to the cabin Eli." "Good" said Eli, "I'll start guttin' the hogs, no sense lettin' good meat go to waste." Jack chuckled and thought, MacGowan, always thinkin' about not lettin' anything go to waste. Jack left for the horse.

Eli made a check on Dawg, threw more wood on the fire, and started to work on the hogs. There were four hogs to bleed out and field dress. Eli started out with the smallest of the group. He wrapped a rope around the hind legs and threw the other end of the rope over a sturdy looking limb. He tugged on the rope and pulled the hog off the ground. He slid his hunting knife from its sheath and in one quick motion, slit the hog's throat. The blood started draining from the critter, turning the snow to crimson.

He grabbed the next one that he thought he could hoist and completed the same process. The last two were too big for him to handle by himself. Eli thought he better let them be for now. He started the job of gutting the feral beasts. Cut a slit down the length of the hogs from rump to gullet. He pulled out the entrails and organs. Eli though he would take only the select chunks, the hams, shoulders and tenderloins. Normally with his hogs, he would not waste anything. Today he would not have time to get everything. Dawg was more important. After he had separated the desired parts from the hogs, he washed them in the branch and hung each to dry. The cold north wind blowing today insured the meat would be good for a long while.

Jack arrived with the horse. He checked on Dawg, who was still in the dream world. Jack said "looks like the bleeding has dried up; time will tell if he makes it."

They built a makeshift hammock from Jack's blanket, slung Dawg onto the side of the horse, and hung as many hog parts as would fit. They kicked out the fire, picked up a ham and shoulder each, and headed back to the cabin.

The walk back was downhill and they wasted no time in getting Dawg back to the warmth of the cabin. Eli and Jack grabbed an end of the sling and gingerly carried him to the cabin. They placed him near the stove on a bed of quilts. Dawg whimpered once but never opened his eyes.

Eli said "Jack will you watch Dawg and I'll go to MacAndrews and get some salve and let them know about the hogs still up on Maggie's Branch." Jack confirmed with a nod.

Eli handed the tenderloins to Jack; he knew he would have them cooked up for supper. He took the rest of the hog meat to the smoke house. He hung two hams up, rubbed the rest of the meat with salt, and packed it in two wood barrels in the smoke house.

Eli slung his old leg over the horse's back and slid into the saddle, slapped the reins and headed for the settlement. Past the cemetery, crossing MacGowan Creek at the two fords, the usual route, but today Eli hardly took notice of the geography. His thoughts were on Dawg.

He remembered the first time he laid eyes on the old mutt. He was just a bundle of fur with two black eyes. He was in a wooden crate on the porch at MacAndrews's Store. Gussie was with Eli, as usual, that day. His became pie eyed as he saw the pup in the crate. He picked up the little fur ball and held him up to admire.

He remembered greeting Corntassel, who sat propped up in a MacGowan straight back chair, on the porch. Corntassel puffed on his pipe and grinned. "That is the last one left Gussie, would make a good huntin' dog for you," said Corntassel.

Gussie's questioning eyes turned toward his father. Eli tried not to look but Gussie was persistent and they locked eyes. "Paw can I have him" asked Gussie. Eli paused and gave Corntassel a look of dismay.

What was he thinking having this mutt out here today? Corntassel had known today was the delivery day for Eli's whisky. Eli thought this was a trap for sure. He thought about the fates of the long line of dogs they had on the MacGowan place. They had all died at an early age, due to run-ins with hogs, bears, snakes, floodwaters, or steel traps. They found their last dog, Jake, a bloody mess after a run in with feral hogs. Eli remembered how Gussie had cried for days over that young mutt.

He studied the situation and spoke. "You can have him boy, but he will *not* be named, you will get attached to him, like Jake, it's bad luck."

Gussie would have agreed to anything to gain the possession of the little pup. "Thanks Paw," said Gussie. Eli said, "You better thank that Indian sittin' there." Gussie said, "Thanks Mister Corntassel." Corntassel nodded with a grin at Gussie.

Eli only shook his head while displaying a faint grin.

So Gussie held true to his father's rule about naming the pup, so he called him Dawg. Eli chuckled, and said to himself, "I reckon Dawg *is* a name after all."

Eli, finished with his daydream, arrived at MacAndrews's Store. He tied the horse and went inside. MacGowan, Corntassel, and Tom Gilliam were sitting by the stove, chewing tobacco.

MacAndrews spat his brown juice into an empty lard can and said, "What brings you into the settlement Eli?"

Eli said, "I need some salve for that old dog."

Corntassel rose and went behind the counter and rummaged around in a box and retrieved a tin of salve. He handed it to Eli and said "two bits." Eli dug for his change bag and concluded the transaction with Corntassel.

Corntassel asked "your dog hurt Eli?" Eli said, "He had a run in with some hogs."

Tom Gilliam spoke "Eli they's been a bunch of hogs rampagin' the edges of the settlement, they got four of my best hens and one rooster last week, I killed one but four or five ran off."

Eli said, "We finished them off, but they might have finished Dawg."

MacAndrews spat and said "Eli there was an Indian by the other day lookin' for you said he was a friend, did he find you?"

Eli nodded in the affirmative and said, "I better get back and see to my dog, and they's two boars field dressed and hung in an oak up on Maggie's Creek. If you know anyone who wants um, take um."

Gilliam said, "I could always use some meat for them youngins', thanks Eli." Eli said "you would need your mule; the one is a big un."

Corntassel inquired to MacAndrews, "all right if I go with Gilliam and get the other hog?" MacAndrews said "yes but you will have to split it with me, since you are workin' today and your absence will put me a bind." Eli looked around the empty store and smiled, he thought that MacAndrews was tighter than the bark on a hickory tree.

Corntassel and Gilliam rode up MacGowan Creek with Eli to the fork with Spring Creek, he told them to take the first branch to the north, which would be Maggie's Branch. Eli rode on to the cabin; it had been a long day.

It was nearly dark when Eli reached the cabin. He tossed the salve to Jack who was standing in the door. Eli said, "Get started Jack while I tend to the animals;" Jack nodded and closed the door.

Eli put up his horse and fed the animals, finished the milking and walked back to the cabin. Both men were hoping for good news about Dawg, but expecting the worse. He thought there has sure been a lot of dying going on around this place.

He opened the cabin door, sat the milk on the table and observed Jack rubbing the salve on Dawg's wounds. Dawg hardly responded to Jacks doctoring work. Eli's heart sank and his eyes filled with tears. This old dog dying would be hard to take, he thought. He was the last connection he had with Gussie and he had promised to take care of him.

"Jack will he make it?"

"Will be close Eli, if he makes it through the night, he might."

Eli took the milk to the springhouse and poured it into the churn. He retrieved a jug of cold milk, walked back to the cabin, a worried man. He entered the cabin and poured some milk into the tin cups, for supper.

Jack had supper ready and although worried, they were tired, hungry, and ready to eat. Eli and Jack ate the tenderloin and biscuits until they could not hold another morsel.

Eli patted his belly and "said it's a shame Dawg can't share the rewards of his good work but there will be plenty later if he's around."

They cleaned up and turned in for the night; Eli on the old corn tick bed and Jack on the feather tick, in Eli and Maggie's bedroom.

CHAPTER ELEVEN
THE REWARD

Eli's dreams that night were vivid and detailed. He dreamed of the day he found out about his land grant. For his service in The Revolution, the government sent Eli a letter, telling him he would receive a parcel of land, called a grant.

He didn't know what the Hiwassee Land Unit, grant, or what range, township, and section meant. These were strange terms to Eli at the time. They would soon come to be very important when he was locating and standing on the corners of his new land.

His sister-in-law, Mollie, also received a grant to a parcel of land in the Hiwassee Unit. Her claim was for her husband Isaac's service in the war. Mollie MacGowan had lawyer draw up papers so Eli could file her claim and register her deed. She would make the trip in the spring to settle her land but was not up to making this trip due to her failing joints.

Eli was anxious to visit the claims and soon made plans to go inspect the new land. He sent word to Jack Mankiller up on Roan Mountain, by his sons Isaac and John, hoping he would make the journey with him. Jack replied two days later by showing up with Isaac and John, on their return. Eli was happy to see Jack; he had not seen him for about a year. Jack was a good man to have by your side when going to a new land.

William MacGowan wanted to make the trip and although Eli knew he would slow them down, he welcomed his father on the trip. It was fall and Eli had his crops in and knew Maggie and the children could handle the chores around the farm, but he wanted to get down and back, before the winter set in.

Eli, Jack and William planned the trip. William had borrowed a map from one of the men in the valley and although a bit out of date, it would give them, the general lay of the land.

They packed up the mules, straddled the horses, and were off. It was a cool crisp October morning, perfect for an adventure Eli thought. Eli barked out a loud "*hah*" and the horses took the first steps in a journey of two hundred miles to the new land.

William was a little long in the tooth for such an arduous trip, but he was still tough and would not let on if he were dying. That is the way of the Scots. They had a discipline hammered into their blood for dozens of generations.

Some said that William MacGowan, if placed on a rock in the Atlantic with a corn seed would thrive. Eli certainly didn't fall far from that tree, the old tree that sat tall on the horse to his right. He was proud of his father and his bloodline, without a doubt.

Eli's party made their way, day after day, through the new towns with muddy streets and big expectations; Greeneville, Newport, to Knoxville where they took the Federal Road to the south. They crossed the Tennessee River, keeping their southwestward course; they crossed the French Broad River at Lowery's Ferry where they spent their sixth night of the trip.

They rose early the next morning, standing around the fire, the coffee not quite ready, Eli scanned his surroundings. He said, "This Tennessee Valley is a fertile land" as he viewed the emerald waters of the French Broad River, to the north and south.

The north was a wide green valley with scattered old Cherokee Settlements to the high mountains that formed the Tennessee and North Carolina divide. To the south, it was a wide green valley as far as his eyes could see. He hoped his lands would be this good.

The rest of his traveling companions stirred; they prepared breakfast and wolfed it down. They cleaned up the mess and started the day. It was another cool October morning, good traveling weather. "We will make good time today," Eli said to his companions. They agreed.

Chatter was limited, while the men were in the traveling mode; matter of fact, chatter was limited all the time. The MacGowans had no history for being very conversant, neither was Jack Mankiller. The clopping of the horses and mules provided most of the sounds outside of nature's own music.

They watched a flock of whooping cranes flying south, must have been a thousand of them, Eli thought. This was a sure sign that winter would be hot on their trail.

Eli thought this was always a good time of year to travel. Weather was usually cool and dry, streams were down and easy to ford, and game was good and easy to find because they had no cover of leaves to hide behind.

This day would end at Nonaburg, they bedded down and since it was Wednesday, they went to the prayer meeting at the Nonaburg Church.

It was good to attend meeting, they had missed services due to their recent traveling. They all went, even Jack, who went for entertainment purposes only. God was a hard sale to Jack Mankiller; Eli often prayed for him, but didn't bother discussing it anymore because he thought Jack was a believer at heart.

The Nonaburg Church service was *lively*. It was a fire and brimstone message delivered by a fiery little man that was about as wide as he was tall. He jumped and shouted, whooped and whirled. The congregation sang "Bringing in the Sheaves" and afterward the preacher asked if anyone in the congregation could read the book. Eli stepped forward and spoke to the congregation in a manner that, anyone who knew him, would have known, inspired words were about to be spoken.

Eli's voice was reverent, loud, and clear and reverberated through every crevice in the little church. Eli said, "We have traveled far from our homes in Washington County, to see the new land that the Lord has provided for us, in McMinn County. He has kept us from harm in our travels, and has provided for our needs."

Eli's father and sons had seen this side of his life, but his words took Jack aback. Jack listened intently, as did the rest of the little congregation.

Eli thought about some scriptures that would be in keeping with their travels. Eli said "I shall read from the Scottish King James Bible; the book of Psalms, chapter one twenty one, verses one through eight." He read, "I'll lift up mine eyes unto the hills, from whence cometh my help. My help cometh from the Lord, which made heaven and earth. He will not suffer thy foot to be moved: he that keepeth thee will not slumber. Behold, he that keepeth Israel shall neither slumber nor sleep. The Lord is thy keeper: the Lord is thy shade upon thy right hand. The sun shall not smite thee by day, nor the moon by night. The Lord shall preserve thee from all evil: he shall preserve thy soul. The Lord shall preserve thy going out and thy coming in from this time forth, and even for evermore." Eli sat, and the congregation said, in unison, "Amen."

The service was over. Eli and his travel mates shook hands with their brothers and sisters of that night. Members of the congregation chatted in the churchyard for a while and dispersed. Eli and crew left early on, because of tired butts and an early morning start.

Eli wondered what Jack's thoughts were on the walk back to camp. They never mentioned salvation since that night.

They arrived in camp and turned in for the day, most were asleep quickly tonight. Eli said his prayers, thought about his family way off in Washington County, and asked the Lord to take care of them tonight and he joined the rest of the group in slumber.

Awakened by the cold morning rain hitting his face, Eli sat up and rubbed his eyes. He had gone to sleep under the millions of stars in the Tennessee sky to wake with nothing but darkness. He blinked his eyes closed, to stop the stinging drops that were striking his exposed eyeballs. The rest of the group stirred quickly as the rain jarred them awake too.

They threw a canvas up over the fire, huddled around to warm, and stirred up some breakfast. Eli guessed it must be about five because there was a little light showing to the east behind the mountains. He shivered himself warm, while again attempting to rub the sleep from his eyes.

They made short work of breakfast, cleaned the pots and pans, packed the gear and headed back on the Federal Road. The road was solid, for the most part, and well maintained, Eli had observed. This day would be a test, for sure.

The road mostly followed the old warpath, that had followed the old buffalo trail, or at least that is what the old man, who ran the Lowery's Ferry, said. Solid or not it would still be a miserable and wet ride today.

Eli and Jack had spent more days than they could count, riding and marching in this sort of weather. Just keep putting one foot in front of the other; he could remember his major saying, on the way to the battle at King's Mountain.

Eli now realized that he was going to get a second reward for that trek. He thought that the gift of independence, to live as a free man, was enough reward, and now he was going to receive the gift of land. He thought that he was fortunate, to live in such a time, and such a country.

He thought that no land would ever compensate for the life of his brother Isaac or the other fine men who died in the war. At least he did not die in vain. His, was a sacrifice that was required, and he knew Isaac would agree, if he were here. Just the same, he thought how fine it would have been, to have Isaac by his side today, making his own claim. Eli guessed having his son Isaac with him, would have to do.

The horses clopped along the miles that day, the rain eased off around mid afternoon. They followed the road down to the Hiwassee River, made a right turn, and followed a path down river to Calhoun. This was where the government clerk would settle his paperwork and Eli would finalize his claim; but it would have to keep until tomorrow because it was near dark, when they arrived.

Calhoun was the county seat of the new county of McMinn, which would soon be Eli's home county. Calhoun, located on the banks of the Hiwassee River was a quaint little town with muddy streets and a few little buildings. Eli could tell this town had dreams of being a larger city, time would tell he thought. Isaac discussed its potential with his father.

Calhoun was certainly no Knoxville, Isaac thought, but he could see a future in this town.

Isaac noticed the general store was doing good business and had a "for sale" sign tacked on the front door. Isaac commented that he would have to talk to the owner.

Isaac owned two general stores back in the Watauga Valley, one in Jonesborough and one in Watauga. He had discussed turning the stores over to his two oldest sons to run and he was looking to expand his business. The boys were practically running things now, anyway.

Isaac liked the looks of Calhoun, maybe this would be a good place to settle down, he thought; he was not much for farming but was well suited for business.

Eli said, "We'll go over and visit with the owner after we get settled in for the night." They thought since the rain was still coming and going they would seek a dry place to bed down for the night.

After inquiring with a man on the muddy streets, he directed the group to a livery. The liveryman said he would bed them in the loft and stable their horses and mules. They bedded down the animals and found a tavern for some supper.

It was good to sit and eat a hot meal. Although it was not Maggie's cooking, it was warm and filling. They all ate and drank their fill of coffee. Eli liked the people here; he thought they were friendly and fair, for town folk.

He asked the tavern owner about the grant office and received directions. He told Eli that there had been several grantees through town since spring; he inquired why Eli was just now claiming his land.

Eli said, "I am concerned that I'll get what is left over, and not wanted." The proprietor smiled and said, "No sir it was a lottery, by numbers. You have what you have, no matter when you claim it."

Eli thought that he was not much on gambling or drawing lots; especially for his land, but he would wait and see what would become of this paper with the strange lines and terms.

Eli, Isaac, and William decided to walk to the general store and talk to the owner. Jack said, "I'll stay at the tavern for a glass or two of whisky." Eli said, "We will see you later", and they headed across the muddy street.

They walked in and Isaac struck up a conversation with the proprietor. He was a seasoned old man, who had most of his days behind him. He was a windy and outgoing man though, who could sell to a dead man.

Isaac said, "Why are you sellin' your store, if you don't mind my askin'." The old man replied, "Not at all, young man. I do not mind in the least. I am ready to settle down with a widow woman up in Knoxville. She has a store, her man has died, and she wants me to sell out and marry her. Think I'll take her up on the offer."

The MacGowans chuckled. Isaac said, "I might want to buy this establishment if you are willin'."

The old man said, "See the sign; it's for sale, make a fair offer and I'll sell it all." He said, "I live up stairs, enough room up there for a good size family. Take a look around if you want."

Isaac said, "I would like to look around and to see your books too." They shook hands and started walking around.

This is where Eli and William made their escape from the store. They headed back to the tavern and retrieved Jack. Eli thought this would be better than getting him out of the lockup in Calhoun, in the morning.

They eventually all congregated at the livery that night.

Isaac said, "I have made a deal with the old man to buy the store. I'll have to the spring to make the purchase."

Eli thought that would work out, with the move in the spring, many things to take care of between now and then he thought.

Eli didn't rest well; his head was full to the brim. Thinking about Maggie and those he left in the Watauga Valley; anxious about what tomorrow held. There were all the dealings with the government agent. He wondered how he would get his family moved here in the spring.

He prayed, and finally went to sleep.

Morning came, Eli had been awake and already had his horse saddled for the visit to the claims office. Jack, and Eli's two sons, Isaac and John, stirred to life.

William didn't wake for a while; they let him rest, because they knew the long trip was wearing on his old bones. After they were all up and dressed, they washed at the horse trough, and when to the tavern for breakfast.

The ham and eggs went down easy; Eli was ready to get his business settled this day. They went back, packed up their gear, settled with the liveryman, and headed the pack towards the Hiwassee Purchase Claims Office in downtown Calhoun.

The government man was sitting in a chair in front of the office, drinking coffee and smoking a pipe.

Eli's crew tied off their animals and Eli stepped onto the porch, extended his huge hand and said, "I am Elijah MacGowan from Washington County, Tennessee."

The government man smiled and said "Jacob Smith, good to make your acquaintance, Mister MacGowan. I see you have some paperwork for me."

"I have been wondering when and *if* you were going to show. I am closing up at the end of the year and there are only a few claims left to settle. Glad you made it, to get what is rightly yours." Eli felt heartened by the agent's courtesy, but allowed that one would not get to be a government man, having a belligerent manner.

Eli followed him inside, Jack and the rest of the MacGowans found a seat on the edge of the porch to wait.

Eli explained his claim papers and showed the papers for his brother Isaac's claim for Mollie. "All the paperwork is in order," said the government man.

Mr. Smith was efficient and to the point. He unrolled a large map and showed Eli where his corners were, and gave him directions to find his land. Eli learned it was fifteen miles to the east to his claim and Mollie's claim was a mile closer. They both had six hundred forty acres, or a section of land, as they called it.

Mr. Smith said, "It is one mile square." Eli thought that was a considerable bit of land. Mr. Smith said "good luck", as he finalized the claim, and gave Eli the deeds.

Eli stopped by the courthouse, a log cabin by the river, to register the deeds; then they stopped by the general store for a few provisions and headed up river to find and investigate his new land.

Eli followed the directions that Smith had given him and they made good time. He reached the creek that he now owned. They followed the creek up to a fork, where they decided to camp for the night. Eli felt at ease this night.

With the morning light, they were off to exploring; to find his four corners, it was not too hard. The slashed and hacked trees the government surveyors had left made the lines clear. Eli and his travel mates hacked more marks along the boundaries to be sure they would remain visible to his neighbors.

Eli was pleased at his land, it was a good mix of mountain and bottomland, plenty enough for hunting, timber, and crops. They studied the lay of the land, and decided on a future cabin site.

The site they picked laid well, good bottomland, by a good clear running creek, a spring flowed plenty of cool water. The ridge to the north would keep the cold north wind away.

They stayed four days, checking out the geography of what would be the new MacGowan place. He continued to be pleased, as were his father and sons.

Jack showed no favor, as he was not much for property. Being a Cherokee, he didn't understand how you could *own* the land, anymore than you could *own* the air. Jack Mankiller, being a drifter, made his home where he slept at night.

The next day they went down to Isaac and Mollie's claim, marked it and located a cabin site, pending Mollie's approval, in the spring.

The next morning they packed up for the long trek back home. Eli allowed as how he would have a lot to do in the winter, getting ready for the move to McMinn County.

They rode and Eli pondered things. They came to the ferry at the settlement called Columbus, on the Hiwassee River. A Cherokee operated the ferry there.

Jack, Eli and the operator conversed in broken Cherokee mixed with English, or at least the Tennessee/Scottish version, of English. They talked and smoked, as the rest of the MacGowan clan rested and smoked. After a good rest, they started back north for Washington County.

The sound of Jack Mankiller closing the stove door jarred Eli awake from his pleasant dream. Jack was up checking on Dawg. He also took time to stuff more wood in the stove's belly.

Eli inquired about Dawg's condition; Jack said, "Still breathin'." Dawg looked peaceful, he was breathing shallow, but still breathing, Eli thought. He went back to bed to continue his pleasant dreams, he hoped.

CHAPTER TWELVE
RAMPS, BEANS, AND A CABIN

The sweet aroma of pork frying roused Eli from his slumber. Jack was hungry and in a cooking mood. Eli thought this would be good for his growling belly. He rolled over to see the old Cherokee at work and was astonished at the site he saw.

There sat Dawg munching on tenderloin, pausing only to slurp some milk, from a bowl. Eli thought he was dreaming, he rubbed his old eyes and refocused on the sight. It was not a dream; Dawg *was* back among the living!

"Well," said Eli, "looks like you have company for breakfast this morning Jack." Dawg didn't acknowledge the comment. Jack only grinned, and continued stirring the gravy.

Eli rose, slipped on his clothes, and strolled over to sit by Dawg. He didn't want to act *too* happy, for fear of making Dawg think he cared about him. Jack said, "He feels well enough to eat, that is for sure", as he handed Dawg another sizable chunk of tenderloin.

Eli said, "it is truly justice that Dawg is eatin' the hog that dern near eat him." Jack grinned, and fed Dawg a biscuit.

Eli thought about rubbing Dawg's head but thought the dried hog blood and slobber would not smell too good on his hands while eating breakfast.

Dawg, apparently full, lay back down on the quilts and closed his eyes. Eli thought he would make it; he just would need a few days to knit back together.

"Jack, what's for breakfast, I'm starvin'," said Eli. "Red, we got tenderloin, eggs, gravy and coffee, ready for the plate and cup" Jack replied.

They ate breakfast and smoked. Eli asked, "Jack do you think we should stay close to the dog today?" Jack said, "If you want me, I'll hang around the cabin today, I can split some wood and keep a close watch on the old dog."

"Good, that will let me check my traps, milk, and feed" said
Eli.

Eli lit out towards the creek and crunched over the frozen
land. Another cold day, Eli thought, will have to keep moving to
keep warm.

Eli did some studying while he was walking. He really liked
having Jack around and wondered if he would stay a while.
Probably not, he thought, Jack is a bit of a wanderer.

Eli reached his first trap, it yielded a mink, he continued to the
next, thinking. If I just ask him to stay, he would not. If I tell him I
need some help, he would not turn me down, in a time of need.
This was Eli's thinking as he completed his trap run, a productive
day, three minks and two muskrats. He laid the animals in the barn,
and went to the cabin to warm.

Jack and Dawg were sitting by the stove, Jack puffing on his
pipe. Dawg acknowledged Eli, barely. Eli was starting to think that
the little loyalty Dawg had for him, was shifting over to Jack. Eli
thought that Dawg was a turncoat anyway and this treatment didn't
surprise him in the least. He was *never* Eli's dog.

Jack inquired, "How did the trappin' go?" Eli gave him the
report, sat, and lit his pipe. Dawg lay back down, and continued to
ignore Eli.

Jack said, "Let's go skin them critters." Eli agreed and they left
for the barn. Dawg walked gingerly, still sore from his guts having
his stuffed back in place, he hung close to Jack's heels, occasionally
glancing at Eli, with a look meant to aggravate. Eli, just as stubborn
as Dawg, tried to ignore the old mutt's insulting glances.

As they arrived at the barn, Eli tried to close the door leaving
Dawg out in the cold; Jack noticed shook his head and grinned. He
let Dawg enter the barn.

Jack inquired to Eli, "Why do you treat the old dog this way?"

Eli said, "I feed him and even let him sleep in the cabin on the
cold nights and he *still* will not be my dog." Jack said, "He *is* your
dog, you old fool. Does he not stay with you? Does he not hunt for

you? You two are just too much alike; you are just like this old dog, Eli. You are too stubborn for your own good."

Jack continued, "You have a good heart Eli, but you have just become a hard man inside. You are my brother and I'll say these things to you, from my heart. You have had bad things happen to you, but they happened to Maggie too. She is broken from losin' them youngins like you are Eli. She is broken from losin' you. Why do you *not* open your eyes and see this? She *needs* you and you *need* her, old friend. Go see her, and I'll stay and tend to the farm. Will you *do this* Eli?"

Eli grew quiet; he knew the words from Jack were true. He knew Jack was trying to fix two broken hearts, but Eli would not have any of his counsel; not right now anyway.

Eli picked up a mink and started skinning it. Jack did likewise. That was all of the conversation, for the rest of the day.

The weeks passed, the north winter winds changed to a soft southerly breeze as spring popped in the Hiwassee Valley. Eli, Jack, and Dawg walked up MacGowan Mountain to dig for ramps, the garlic of the mountains. They dug half a dozen ramps, some ginseng roots, sassafras, yellow roots, and jimson weed.

Even Dawg would not get near this smelly collection. The ramps were a strong tasting, and even stronger smelling bulb that was best cut up in stews or cooked with eggs. Ramps would make ones breath smell foul beyond words, for days after consuming, with or without eggs.

The brewing and drinking a tea from jimson weed was good for headaches. The same tea made from yellow root and sassafras would cure the bellyache. Eli dried and sold Ginseng, at MacAndrews's Store but had no way of knowing that the humble mountain products he harvested and brewed, ended up sent all over the world.

The ginseng went to China; the chestnuts Eli collected in the fall, either ended up in the bellies of his hogs or ended up roasting on the streets of New York at Christmas. Eli's Scotch whisky, only sold locally, but would have been welcomed anywhere in the world.

Eli and Jack sacked up their herbs, walked over to Deep Gap, where they found suitable rocks and sat, lit their pipes and puffed for a while. They admired the sight before their old eyes.

The leaves were just starting to form which gave the mountains an emerald green cast. The chestnuts were in full bloom, the white blossoms gave the mountains the look of a spring snow. They just sat and took it in, without speaking.

They watched a black bear coming up the trail. Dawg was off Eli stood and whistled twice. Dawg stopped a hundred feet from the young boar bear. Eli thought he didn't want to spend the rest of the day stuffing dog entrails and sewing dog hide together.

Dawg was probably hoping that Eli and Jack would stop him, before he had to make good, on his threatening growls.

The bear backed down the trail a ways and Dawg took a few steps toward Eli and Jack. Eli said, "Get back here Dawg." Dawg finally walked back to the old men. They all watched the frightened young bear lope back down the ridge. The excitement was over, Dawg lay back down; Eli and Jack lit up their pipes again.

"Jack," said Eli, "I sure could use your help around here, with me bein' by myself. If you would be a mind to stay, we could put up a cabin for you."

Eli continued with his hopeful invitation to his old friend, "Jack, how 'bout you find a place you like here and we'll get started."

Jack said nothing for a good while, studying the offer from his friend. Jack thought how he *was* getting old and his traveling days would soon be over. Maybe settling down in one spot would not be too bad.

In his usual mischievous manner, Jack grinned and said, "Are you gettin' tired of my cookin' Eli?" Eli only shook his head no, and waited for a serious response from Jack.

"Red, we are too old to build a cabin," said Jack. "We can get help from the settlement when we need it," said Eli. Jack thought some more and spoke, "I think I'll take you up on that offer, Red."

"Well," said Eli, "now is a good time to get started, before its time to get the crops in the ground. We have about two or three weeks to get the chestnut logs cut and brought down."

"Do you have a site picked out, that will do? Anywhere on my land, is yours for the takin'," said Eli. Jack said "how 'bout over on Maggie's Branch, on the edge of your cornfield."

Eli said, "There's a spring there," "I noticed," said Jack. "Well, there are about enough good chestnut trees, close by there to build a cabin," said Eli.

Eli said, "it is done, we will start in the mornin'." Eli slapped Jack on the back. "It will be good to have you as my neighbor, my friend, good indeed," said Eli.

They headed back down the mountain and shot a couple of squirrels for supper, along the way. Eli and Jack stepped a little lighter or so it seemed. Eli looked forward to building something again and Jack was to have his first home.

Eli could not contain his happiness at this turn of events, as was obvious by the smile that stayed on his face, for the entire trip back to the cabin.

Jack fried up the squirrels with the fresh ramps and along with dried beans, he had left cooking all day; it made for a good supper. Eli stirred up some corn cakes; they ate their fills and turned in for the day.

Jack awakened the next morning to a foul smell. A smell caused his eyes to water and his nose to burn. He pondered, in a half-sleepy fog, what this could be.

Then Eli heard Dawg emit a sound accompanied by a foul aroma. Jack started playing his own foul tune, while standing at the stove, cooking breakfast. Then Eli joined in and blew out a foul cloud of his own.

"What vile things have we ate?" bellowed Eli. "We need not have ramps and beans anytime soon, if we are stayin' inside."

Jack laughed and let go with another burst. Eli laughed and did the same as he ran for the door and flung it open. He breathed in deeply, the cold fresh mountain air. It was nothing like the putrid air that occupied the confines of the cabin. Jack laughed again.

After the men had cleared their bowels of this foulness and fresh air had replaced the stench inside the cabin; they sat down to eat a big breakfast and talk about building Jack Mankiller's cabin.

Eli pushed the breakfast plates to one side and started sketching out the plans for the cabin. He took a piece of chalk and scratched some crude lines on a slate tablet. He made a plan that had a front room with fireplace and kitchen and side room for sleeping.

Eli asked, "Jack what about this?" Jack pondered the design and nodded in the affirmative. "You will need a cellar to store your taters, onions and such," said Eli. Jack agreed and added, "A sleepin' loft would be good for company."

Eli stood up and said, "Let's go find a spot for the cabin, Jack." Dawg rose and let another burst of bean and ramp gas go in front of Eli. Jack laughed, Eli grabbed the slate tablet and they darted out of the cabin and for Maggie's Branch and fresher air.

The sun was just up over the ridge as they arrived. The wagon was loaded with all the saws, axes, mauls, wedges and ropes they would need for the day. The oxen pulled the wagon and Jack rode the mule, all the tools and animals met the requirements for the task.

Eli said "Jack you find a good spot and let's get started." Jack paced around, looked over the site. He sized up the lay of the land, which way would get the most light in the winter and least sun in the summer.

He walked repeatedly, making a smaller circle until he stopped and said, "We will build here." Eli walked around and grinned. "This is good Jack, so the front goes here," he asked while waving his arms to the side. Jack nodded as Dawg barked his approval. They both laughed, and clasped their hands together. Eli said "well, let's get to work."

Work they did, with two men on the crosscut saw they started making the nice chestnuts and white oaks fall. Chestnuts were just right for the cabin about two feet across, they would make the walls of the cabin. The white oaks would make the shakes for the roof. They laid down all the trees in the cabin spot and sawed the logs into lengths as needed. They lay the logs aside to allow the stumps to be grubbed. Once the grubbing was finished, they retrieved their dinner from the wagon, sat, and ate.

Eli brought out the slate and chalk and started to figure the details for the cabin. Jack had his input too. They both had serious looks as the discussion boiled down to the final details. Like what size to make the porch and where to put the windows and such.

They worked together like a good team of mules these two. If questioned it is doubtful that they could remember ever really arguing about anything of real substance. They enjoyed each other's company and felt at ease working together.

They finished their plans, laid the slate and chalk aside and went back to work. They knew they would have to dig the cellar before laying the foundation logs. They broke out the picks and spades and started digging.

The ground was soft in this mountain cove, so the digging was easy for the first few feet. Then they hit the hard rubble and sandstone. This made for a considerable bit of effort to finish the cellar.

They had about half the cellar finished and Jack said, "It is time to call it a day." He would scratch up some supper as Eli tended his chores.

Supper went down easy as the two old friends ate and drank. They smoked a bit, cleaned up the pots and plates and went to bed.

"We will not need anyone to rock us to sleep tonight," Eli said. Jack grunted a response as he crawled into his bed. Eli thought that maybe they should get some help, he would think on that. For the two old men and Dawg, sleep came early and easy this night.

CHAPTER THIRTEEN
ON THE MEND

Eli, Jack and Dawg rose from their slumber, ate breakfast and made plans for the day. Eli said, "I think I'll go to the settlement and see about getting' some help for the cabin." Jack smiled and replied, "I think that will be a good idea Red, we are just two and too old." Dawg barked his approval, he was getting tired of watching the two old timers work, it was wearing him out, besides he knew there would not be any hunting until this cabin work was finished.

Jack said, "I'll stay and work on the cellar, after I get these skillets washed up." Dawg stayed with Mankiller.

Eli mounted his horse and headed to the settlement. During his journey to the settlement, Eli thought how he would start the cabin. He planned to avoid some of the mistakes of his experiences in cabin building. His experience building dozens of cabins, through the years, made him valuable around the settlement. Eli was valued and often sought out for his skills.

Eli also studied what Jack had not so subtlety mentioned to him about patching up with his family. Eli missed Maggie, his sons, and his grandchildren. He thought how he was to blame for the shape his life was in these days. He was thinking about it now. That was a start.

He hitched up to the rail at MacAndrews Mercantile. Corntassel and MacAndrews sat on the porch and greeted Eli. "What brings you in to town this time of the month Eli," inquired MacAndrews. Eli said, "I am lookin' for some help with a cabin I'm buildin' for Jack Mankiller."

MacAndrews said "he gonna stick around, I guess." Eli nodded yes and asked, "Know of any good workers that I can use?"

Corntassel said, "They's plenty of MacGowans around this valley, why don't you ask them?" Eli didn't respond, but thought, *another meddler*; Jack was not enough to listen to, *now* Corntassel. He thought that he didn't recollect the Cherokees being that much of peacemakers, but he had two to deal with now.

Eli didn't acknowledge, aloud, Corntassel's comment, but said,

"Well, if you hear of any men who ain't afraid of hard work, tell them to come up Maggie's Branch and they will find us. I'll pay a fair wage for fair labor."

He went into the store and picked up some tobacco, nails, hinges, and glass to make windows. He watched as MacAndrews carefully wrapped the glass panes while Corntassel placed the other items in Eli's canvas bag.

"See you men later," said Eli and he gingerly fastened the glass to the saddle and mounted and left.

As Eli rode up the road, MacAndrews and Corntassel cast a puzzled look at each other. "Eli was a bit talkative today don't you think Corntassel?" said MacAndrews. "Yep, right chatty I would say," replied the Indian. MacAndrews and Corntassel watched Eli ride out of sight and sat, chewing and spitting tobacco juice off the edge of the porch. MacAndrews said,"Corntassel, its slow today, how about you ride over the George MacGowans place and let him know Eli needs some help with a cabin."

Corntassel seemed puzzled by the sudden generosity of the tight wad MacAndrews. Then he thought, another cabin to build, more supplies to sell. Corntassel grinned and said, "It would be a good day for a ride. Think I will."

Corntassel rode up in the fields of George MacGowan's place. George and his younger sons were plowing with two teams of mules attached to turning plows. Corntassel thought that William and Eli MacGowan were present in all these young men. They were tall, strong and straight.

They nodded, to acknowledge his arrival, but didn't stop working. Corntassel dismounted and tied his mule up and walked towards George.

George grinned and walked to meet Corntassel. He offered his hand and the Indian shook it and winced. Corntassel's grip was no match for the vise like hand clamped around his. George released his grip and said, "Welcome Corntassel, what can I do for you?"

Corntassel, stood for a minute, pawed the ground and thought how he could bring up the question about helping Eli with the cabin.

Corntassel said, "Good lookin' ground here George."

George scanned the land with a look of reverence and replied, "Yes, we are blessed with good land and good strong sons to work the fields. I thank the Lord and my Aunt Mollie every day for givin' us her land grant. She told me she was happy that some good came from my Uncle Isaac's death at King's Mountain."

George smiled and said "Corntassel, I figure you didn't ride out here to admire my plowed ground."

Corntassel finally built up his grit and said, "I'll just come out with it, your Paw came to the store this mornin' and asked if we knowed anyone who could help build a cabin."

"Why is he buildin' *a cabin?*" George questioned.

Corntassel said, "Him and Jack Mankiller are tryin' to build a cabin, up on Maggie's Branch, that's what he told MacAndrews and me just an hour ago."

George looked at the ground a bit and said, "Thanks for comin' Mister Corntassel; I'll have to ponder and pray on that a bit."

Corntassel thought that the raising had been proper by Eli and Maggie MacGowan and it showed in his sons. Eli should be proud of them; he had never heard an ill word spoken of the MacGowan name. That was truly something to be proud of, not that Eli or Maggie would speak of being prideful.

"I better get back," said Corntassel, "you know how MacAndrews is; he is countin' the minutes for sure."

They both laughed and Corntassel mounted up and returned to the store feeling that he had done a good deed. He only hoped the MacGowans would not let him down.

George went back to relieve a son behind the plow. He did some of his best thinking while plowing and he had some serious thinking to do today.

Eli arrived back at the cabin site, dismounted and tied his horse. Jack and Dawg were in the hole that would be Jack's cellar.

Jack said, "Did you get any help?" Eli said, "Maybe, I planted a seed," Jack looked confused. "What do you mean planted a seed, Eli?"

Eli said, "well, let's just say we will have some help comin' in the mornin'. We need to get this cellar finished up old friend. Crop time will be here before you can blink. They both started digging with picks and spades in earnest."

They paused for a minute and Jack just stood there for a bit, he thought he saw a little grin on Eli's face. He rubbed his chin, and thought tomorrow would provide the answer to this mystery. Eli just grinned and said, "Back to diggin'."

They finished the cellar, set the rocks around the perimeter for a footing and laid the foundation logs into place. They cut the joist logs that would support the floor. "That was a good bit of work, this is a good stoppin' place Jack", said Eli.

"I had better get the chores tended to, if you will fix us some supper Jack," Eli said. This had become a nightly routine lately. Eli doing the chores and Jack cooking seemed like a good deal to Eli.

Eli could not resist taking a parting jab at Dawg and sarcastically said "Dawg don't you overdo it goin' back to the cabin. I hate to see a dog worked to death."

Jack smiled, shook his head, and proceeded on to the cabin. Dawg didn't justify the comment with a response, pulled close to Jack, and joined him for the trip to the cabin.

After supper, Eli and Jack loosened their breeches to allow room for the big supper now expanding in their bellies.

They lit up the pipes to relax for a while. Conversation was sparse and the labor of the day had taken its toll on the two old timers. In a bit, they dozed off to nap, still propped up in their chairs, pipes smoking.

Eli was startled awake to the sound of Jack hopping around the cabin shouting, *"I'm on fire! I'm on fire!"*

Eli noticed that, during his slumber his pipe had fallen from his mouth and landed on the floor in front of him and had burned out.

Jack had not been so fortunate. His pipe had fallen down the front of his shirt to his privates and had apparently started a small brush fire there. He was hopping around the cabin like a mad man, pulling his breeches off. He grabbed the water bucket and threw it on his manhood.

Eli was by this time falling off his chair onto the cabin floor, laughing so hard he could hardly catch his breath.

Jack initially didn't see any humor in the situation and especially didn't see any reason for Eli to laugh at his misfortune. After a closer examination and seeing no permanent damage, Jack began to laugh too.

They both belly laughed to the point of tears running down their old faces. They laughed for a good five minutes and sat down to rest from the ordeal.

"Whew," said Jack, "it has been a long time since I have laughed that hard." Eli chuckled his concurrence and said, "it was quite a show there Jack. Will your rooster live to fight another day?"

After a thorough inspection to insure no residual fire was burning, Jack pulled his breeches back up. "I think my rooster will live to crow again and my eggs are not cooked either."

They roared with laughter again as Dawg sat, with a puzzled look, at these two old coots, acting like schoolboys. Dawg had to think he was the most intelligent being in the cabin tonight. He was probably right.

The excitement over for the evening, they put out the lamp and hit the tick. Sleep soon followed.

Eli hardly closed his eyes when he stirred from a good night's sleep and saw that Jack had breakfast ready for the table. What has got into me Jack; I have took to sleepin' to daylight. He rolled over, put his clothes on, and slid his feet into his overly worn leather boots.

"Are you ready to eat Eli, "asked Jack. "Let me visit the porch first" he replied, as he walked onto the porch and relieved himself. He heard a noise in the distance and gave his brain a few seconds to figure out what the sound was. It was the sound of axes and saws working on trees.

He looked for Dawg; he was not around. "Jack have you seen that mangy mutt?" Jack said, "He is over at the cabin site I think with the hired help. They showed up at daylight as I was fixin' to start breakfast. You snored through the whole thing."

"Well, wonder who MacAndrews sent?" Eli asked. "Let's eat and go find out," said Jack. They made quick work of breakfast, geared up the animals, loaded the tools and took off for Maggie's Branch.

As they neared Jack's future home, Eli could see a considerable bit of work going on. There were trees falling up the ridge and around the field. There were chips flying making notches in the log joints. There were saws singing, as they cut the logs to length. An industrious group for sure; but who were they?

As Eli rode up to the cabin, tears welled up in his eyes. He could see Jack, although grinning, was in the same condition.

There working was George, Robert, Timothy, and Thomas MacGowan, Eli's sons that lived on his brother Isaac's lands. They didn't come alone but brought two or three of their grown or nearly grown sons to help.

There was no doubt of the MacGowan bloodline here, he saw red haired men with big strong bodies working hard. George and Robert were in charge of the cabin construction while his sons Timothy and Thomas were directing the timber cutting work.

George MacGowan walked over to his father and said we heard you and Jack needed a hand. We figured we would not let our father buy labor, when he has sons to help. Eli only nodded agreement, picked up his tools, and went to work directing the operation.

Jack grinned at George and they knew things were on the mend, more than likely Eli had made the first move yesterday. They knew how savvy Eli could be. Jack figured Eli had known his sons would get word and come. Eli was right, as usual.

The MacGowan men worked as if the years had not passed since they had seen their father. Just picked up where their relationship had left off prior to the Yellow Fever days.

Eli was as happy as he had been in years. He looked at Jack Mankiller and knew that he had been sent to make things right and Eli would never forget his help. A cabin seemed a small reward thought Eli.

Chips and sawdust flew as the MacGowans and Jack cut and laid the logs to be hewn and dovetailed. Once the pattern was set, window and door openings established, Eli took four of his grandsons aside and taught them how to make the white oak shakes for the roof. It would take hundreds to cover the cabin and with his supervision, he expected they would make good progress on this first day.

George and sons worked on the foundation and hearth for the fireplace and started bringing the chimney stones up with each layer of logs.

Eli's daughter in laws rolled up in two wagons at dinnertime. The boy's wives all cried tears of joy, hugged Eli and said they were glad to see him again.

They set out a spread of fried chicken, biscuits, sweet potatoes, and buttermilk. Then for dessert, they gorged on fried apple pies. Eli had not eaten like this since Maggie left.

Then they handed him a special gift, it was his newest great granddaughter. A big toothy grin, that they had always loved to see, washed across Eli's face.

Her name is Maggie, her young mother said. Eli said "Little Maggie for sure", as Eli gazed into her blue eyes and stroked her flaming red hair. He sat on the wagon and enjoyed this baby girl most of the afternoon, oblivious to the work going on around him. Jack and the boys were amazed, but happy for Eli.

The afternoon went in a hurry; progress was visible on the cabin. The walls were half completed and the notches for the windows and doors snapped Eli to attention.

He needed to get started building the windows, cabin door and cellar door. That would be his task in the morning, get to the workshop and build windows and doors. He certainly didn't want to slow down the progress on the cabin.

George MacGowan came to his father and said "Paw we will see you in the morning." The other "boys" nodded and grinned their concurrence with George.

Eli grinned back and said, "You boys head towards home and I'll put the tools in the barn." He patted each son and grandson on the back, as each passed by on the way to the wagons. Eli didn't say much; neither did his sons, which was just the MacGowan way, after all.

Jack just stood and observed, grinning with amazement.

Jack said, "Thank you all for the help, there is more for tomorrow." They all smiled. They were tired but would be ready to go in the morning. After all, this was just another routine day of labor.

Dawg observed the work and made sure he marked each wagon before they left the cabin site.

Eli and Jack watched the MacGowan "boys" head down the new wagon path they had formed today. The trail ran around the edge of one of Eli's cornfields to a new ford on Maggie's Branch and on to the MacGowan Creek Road, which Eli had cut with his wagon and cart over the years.

Eli said, "It's gettin' to be a regular town up here, roads a runnin' everywhere." Jack laughed and started loading tools into Eli's wagon.

As they headed back to the barn, they discussed the goings on of the day. Eli said, "We have made a good dent in this cabin today, Jack." Jack nodded his agreement.

It was a good day.

Eli said, "I never thought we would be ready for the winders and doors already. This has caught me by surprise and I guess playin' with little Maggie all afternoon, stole my intention to work."

Eli said, "We are goin' almost too fast, we are ahead of where I thought we would be now. I figured to have some rainy days to build winders and doors. I'll need to get to work on 'em tomorrow mornin'."

Jack grinned and said, "Eli, you need to spend more time with them youngins and slow down a little on the workin'."

Jack grinned and said, "Eli you made headway on more things than the cabin today."

Eli nodded, and went back to talking of only the cabin. "Jack can you go to MacAndrews Store and get some putty for the winders in the mornin'?" Jack said, "I'll go after breakfast and be back to help soon as I can."

They did chores, ate and turned in for the day. Hoping for a good night's sleep and an early rise, a heap of work to do tomorrow they both thought.

Dawg only thought of tenderloin and biscuits for breakfast, the snoring soon started.

CHAPTER FOURTEEN
MOVIN' DOWN THE VALLEY

Once again, Eli was in blissful slumber on the old corn shuck bed. He drifted back through the fog into the spring that they moved from the Watauga Valley, to his land grant, in McMinn County.

It was a cool wet spring that year, the winter was clinging to the snowy mountaintops still. Eli had spent the most of the winter getting ready for the move. There was much to do and he wanted things to go in an orderly way. Eli and his eldest son, Isaac, had made two trips back and forth to Calhoun and his new lands. They spent the spring, summer, and fall getting everything worked out for the eventual transplantation of his family to the new land. Each trip seemed longer than the previous one, as the winter closed in on the valley.

The trips allowed Isaac to settle the details of the store he purchased in Calhoun and to haul the family possessions to be stored in Isaac's store loft.

In the spring, the time came to load the wagons for the final trip to McMinn County. It was a bittersweet time. Isaac's two oldest sons would stay and run the stores in Washington County. All of his sons and daughters except his two youngest daughters would stay put. This part of the move was the hardest on the MacGowan family, separation was a part of life but it was surely not an easy part.

Eli and Maggie's sons, Elijah or Lidge as he they called him, to distinguish him from his father; would stay on his farm in Washington County. So would sons James, a farmer; William, a surveyor; and Jack, a blacksmith. Daughters Sarah, married to farmer John Williams and Gillian, married to Tom White, the postmaster in Watauga, stayed behind with their families.

Mollie, being bed ridden, frail and in poor health, could not make the trip and endure the disruption to her life. She decided to give her 640-acre grant to Eli's sons George, Robert, Timothy, and Thomas. They would all move with their young families to the new land. Mollie weakly said, "I know that your Uncle Isaac would have been happy that Eli's sons will live on his land, I miss him to this day, I'll soon join him. Make good use of the reward of his sacrifice to this nation and family, my good boys. I'll be with you in spirit as I know Isaac will be." There were tears shed and hugs made over her decision.

Maggie hugged Mollie and they cried for a long while. Once the tears had subsided, Maggie spoke to her best friend in this world, "Mollie, if I didn't know that my sons and daughters would be here to care for you, I would not leave. I'll miss you more than I can say, Mollie. You have been like a sister to me all my life. It will be hard to leave you here, I'll miss havin' you to talk with."

Mollie smiled and said, "Maggie MacGowan, you are truly an angel and I'll not see you again, in this life, but I'll see you in my heavenly home when your time comes. Isaac and I'll watch for your comin' and pray it will be a long time from now. Enjoy your family Maggie, you have earned that, do not worry about me anymore, now hug me and be on your way." They hugged, Maggie turned away, never to see Mollie again, in this life, anyway.

Mollie died days later, peacefully in her sleep. She joined Isaac in their cabin in the sky, next to the MacGowans, who were there, where they had staked out their claim on some good bottomland in heaven.

Newton and Lemuel, Eli's youngest sons, decided to pass on the free land offered by their Aunt Mollie and would take advantage of more free land in North Georgia and join in on the gold rush in Dahlonega.

Daughters Gwen and Mattie, and son Gussie moved to the new land with Eli and Maggie.

Eli and Maggie's parents would stay in Watauga.

This was the splintering of Eli and Maggie's family. Eli had been through this already with his brothers and sisters, as had Maggie. Some moved to lands in Kentucky, others to Ohio, and others to Missouri. Land in this new nation was like ripe peaches, just pick what you want and enjoy, thought Eli. Although he ached from the separation from his sons and daughters, he knew that was life, in this raw new land.

The wagons were loaded and ready, on that sad day as Eli and Maggie; not only were they leaving their aged parents and Mollie, but some of their children and grand children.

Eli's mother prayed for a safe journey. She had never been out of the valley in her adult life and she could only fear the worst lay beyond the mountains. She would leave William in his new grave of only months. She feared this trip would be too much for her frail body, but Eli and Maggie insisted,

Eli's mother, Sarah MacGowan, sat in their wagon, waiting to travel with their youngest son to the new lands he had acquired.

Eli said with his voice cracking, "it's time to go" and the wagons rolled away from the MacGowan lands. The wagon train meandered out of the upper valley that day.

Maggie looked back and watched her cabin get smaller and then disappear behind the ridge. They rode by the hilltop home of the MacGowan Cemetery where Eli's father, grandparents, Angus and Gullie lay beside four of their children.

Eli nodded a salute to his grandparents who had brought the MacGowan name to this valley. He fought back the tears and could not swallow down the knot in his throat. He thought how proud they would have been of the group that originated with them.

The MacGowan clan rode by the church where Eli and Maggie were married; past the old Tom Walker place where Dragging Canoe killed Becky Walker, Jack Mankiller's only love. It was a journey of sentiment and sadness.

Maggie wept most of the first day. She worried that she would not see her children again. Maybe she was correct.

It was a long trip, Eli thought, this would be his forth ride to the Hiwassee Valley. He knew this would be a long one with the young children along. Eli hoped he was doing right; time would tell he thought. He prayed for a safe trip and that he was following the right course in making this move.

The trip was uneventful except for the occasional broken wheel or muddy stretch of road. When it rained, they stayed under the canvas as best they could, but mostly they were wet.

At night, they lay under the big starry sky, and listened to the whippoorwills and owls sounding off in the distant night.

During the day, Eli enjoyed watching his family enjoying the sites of the new rivers, towns and mountains they passed along the way. The younger children looked awed at the ferry crossings, and fords along the way. Eli felt his mother was doing well on the trip; he could see a smile on her face, now and then and hoped this would help her grieving, over his father.

It was raining when they reached Knoxville. Eli thought he would treat everyone to a stay at a livery loft and a bought meal for supper.

The livery was meager lodging, but they stayed dry and could spread their blankets and quilts on the hay and sleep well. It was a treat to the entire party and made for a livelier start to the next day.

The morning arrived as a bright sunny spring day. It boosted the morale of the travelers. Maggie cooked breakfast over an open fire built outside the livery. They ate and loaded up the wagons to resume the trip.

They rolled down State Street, a muddy rutted route through the middle of Knoxville. They were impressed at the sight of the Blount College, located on the rise overlooking the Tennessee River, near White's Fort.

Eli and Maggie talked about how they wished that her children could have the means to go to a college, but they knew it was only a dream.

They passed by the Blount Mansion, the home of the former governor of Tennessee, Willie Blount. Admiring the mansion, Maggie said, "I can't believe that people live like this, Eli. Eli said, "I would take my cabin in the mountains any time," as he patted Maggie on the hand. "It is the people in the house that makes it what it is, not the show you see from the street." Eli continued, "A feller told me on our first trip to Knoxville that the buildings on the side of the house are called wings. I thought it would take a heap of flappin' to get that house off the ground."

Maggie laughed, as did the children.

They rattled down the wagon road, only stopping to get the

wagons unstuck in the muddy ruts. This section of the road, as Eli relayed to Maggie was a bad stretch, due to the number of wagons using it.

They only made it as far as Campbell's Station Inn, that night. They stretched the canvas between the wagons ate and bedded down the animals, then the children. This allowed Eli and Maggie time to sit by the fire and talk.

Maggie, reflecting on the events of the day, snuggled with Eli as he wrapped a quilt around both. "Eli," Maggie said, "I think this valley is startin' to fill up, there are so many people comin' and goin'."

Eli smiled and replied, "We are headed to open land Maggie, you will see in a few days. It is a good place we go to, a good place to put down new roots."

"Do we have to cross this river tomorrow Eli?" Maggie asked with dread in her voice. Eli smiled and pulled her closer, "We will not make the crossin' tomorrow, but will on the next. The road will be better and less worn from here on south. There is a ferry across the French Broad River, run by a good man, we will be safe."

They didn't say much, only enjoyed the time they shared under the stars on road to a new home. Eli checked on the fire and Maggie checked on the children before laying down for a welcome rest.

The morning came, the wheels rolled early, and the excitement was alive in the children. They knew a new adventure and new sights were just around the next turn in the road. Eli and Maggie only wanted to get to their destination. Get there and get started on the massive chore that lay ahead.

The day passed as the most uneventful one on the journey. The solid bed of the Federal Road allowed good progress, and as Eli had said, they camped on the north bank of the French Broad River.

The children gazed wide eyed at the sight of this huge ribbon of water that served as the main lifeline to the valley. They saw rafts of travelers heading down the river and watched as the last ferry crossing of the day brought wagons to their side of the river unloaded and tied off for the night.

Eli directed the placement of the wagons for the night; they ate supper and chatted with some of the other travelers. Everyone was tired from the day's journey and talk was polite but brief.

Eli remembered how the children fought their sleep because of the events of the next morning. They had crossed rivers on ferries but had never seen a river of this size.

Maggie shared the excitement of the children, and wanted to talk but Eli had made the crossing several times and was ready for sleep. His last memory of the day was Maggie talking to him as drifted into the dreamland.

The day broke as Eli was waiting in line to board the ferry for the first crossing of the day. Everyone was up early, fed and ready to go. The ferry operator was ready at first light too; he collected the fare from Eli and pulled his loading ramp into place. He directed Eli to start pulling forward onto the ferry.

The creaking of the ferry was not too comforting to Maggie but she trusted Eli and knew he would not place anyone in a harmful place. Once loaded the ferry was on its journey to the south bank of the French Broad. Strong ropes tied to mules on each shore pulled the ferry, and the strong men at each corner used long poles to keep the vessel on its true course.

The bobbing of the ferry, left Maggie feeling queasy and she closed her eyes for most of the crossing. The children on board were excited and laughing all the way across.

As the ferry ground to its destination, on the other bank, Maggie said, "Whew, Eli I am glad to touch land again." Eli chuckled, continued to hold Maggie's hand while the ferryman tightly anchored the old barge in place.

The ramp now in position, the wagons rolled back onto the hard surface of the Federal Road, maneuvered around the waiting northbound wagons and stopped to reposition the contents.

Maggie took this opportunity to find a patch of woods with several of the girls in tow. They soon returned feeling like new people, ready for another leg of the trek.

The party reached Nonaburg Church. It was Wednesday, prayer meeting night. The church members remembered some of the MacGowans, especially Eli. They still remembered his reading of the scriptures.

Eli introduced his family to the congregation, they enjoyed the lively service, and he treated the church to another reading of the scriptures. The services were a welcome social and spiritual event to all in the MacGowan party; was good break from the grind of the trip.

They all slept especially well that night.

The morning came and the wagons started rolling to the south. They made good time and at the end of the day, they could see the distant mountain that was partly theirs.

Maggie was excited to be near to the end of the trip and she encouraged Eli, by telling him that this was a beautiful place and that he had done the proper thing.

Eli thought Maggie always knew the right thing to say to lift him when he was feeling down or doubting himself. She was a special woman and he thanked the All Mighty often for sending her to him.

The boys killed a young doe and dressed her for supper. Maggie and the girls prepared a stew of fresh venison, potatoes, cornbread, and onions. It was the best meal of the journey.

Eli promised them all that tomorrow they would sleep on MacGowan land. It was welcome news to every ear.

There was some fidgeting that night but sleep came eventually to all.

Daylight came and the wagons were loaded and rolling to the new MacGowan lands. Even the oxen, horses and the old sows and cows stepped lively today; Eli wondered if they knew they were almost at the end of the journey too.

They stopped at the settlement and bought some boards, nails, and dry goods they would need to get started.

They loaded up and rolled up the Hiwassee River; Maggie said it was the prettiest river she had ever seen. It was clear as glass, rolling wide with white peaks from the rapids. It had a roar that they heard long before they saw its waters. They followed it up to a clear wide creek; Eli pulled the wagon to a halt.

Eli stepped off the wagon seat, walked over to Maggie and reached for her to join him. As her feet touched the ground, Eli said, "Maggie you are home, this is MacGowan land, we will grow old, die and be buried in its soil."

Maggie looked at the clear running mountain creek where it ran into the Hiwassee River. She smiled for a moment and started to cry. "Eli'" Maggie said, "This is the most wondrous place I have ever seen."

"What is the name of this beautiful creek, Eli?" Maggie asked.

Eli stood and looked up and down the reach of the stream, as far as he could see, and replied, "I reckon we can call it whatever we want to."

Maggie said, "Well, then it will be called MacGowan Creek from this day forward."

Eli paused for a moment then reached and swept Maggie into his arms, waded into the middle of the creek and shouted as loud as he could, "This *is* MacGowan Creek!"

Most of the travelers joined with their father and mother and cheered "MacGowan Creek!"

The Eli's mother stayed on the edge and held on to the little ones, but still laughed, shouted, and praised The Almighty for giving them a safe journey.

Eli paused and observed the wondrous site and thought of Angus and Gullie MacGowan when they arrived in America. Must have been the same feeling he thought. He smiled and thanked them in his thoughts.

They all celebrated for a good while, they made camp and put on a feast, they broke out the bagpipes and fiddles, danced jigs until too tired to dance.

Eli broke up the celebration as he stood in the light of the campfire. He told the revelers, "We have many long weeks ahead, and we have cabins, barns, smokehouses, and springhouses to build. We have fields to clear and plant, if we are not to freeze and starve this winter." He picked up Maggie and swung her around in a circle and they laughed like two children, the children laughed.

It was a good time.

In his dream, the morning came; Eli woke to the sound of the river rolling and watched the stars dim as the sun painted the sky a brilliant orange. He felt Maggie's warm body curled against him and he thought life was good. He felt excited about the coming months; he looked forward to building the new buildings with his sons.

Maggie stirred, and opened her eyes to see Eli looking at her. She smiled and said,"Mornin' Elijah." We are here on our new land. Are you ready for what lies ahead?"

Eli smiled back and said," I'm as ready as a man can be Maggie, ready as a man can be."

They rose and had a big breakfast, loaded the wagons and headed into the heart of the new MacGowan land. Eli headed up MacGowan Creek, followed it to the place he had marked for the cabin. He stopped the wagon and helped Maggie down.

They stood and admired the land; Eli said "we are home Maggie." She dropped to her knees and kissed the rich soil of the Hiwassee Valley, MacGowan soil.

They all stood in admiration of the quality of this site, and then Eli clapped his hands together and said, "Let's get to work."

They wasted no time unpacking the saws, axes, churns, water buckets, and cooking utensils. Items they would need to survive during the cabin raising.

Isaac and family spent the night.

In the morning, they headed to Calhoun with plans of

unloading his wagons before dark. They would shuttle Eli and the other boys' things as soon as they had a barn and cabin built. There was much to do and time was wasting. Eli's mother would stay with Isaac, until the cabin was ready.

They built Eli and Maggie's cabin first, then the barn. Then some would plow and put in crops as the others built one cabin and barn after another. By early fall all the construction on the cabins and barns were finished, the crops were in, the whisky still was operational, and a *celebration* was in order.

Eli invited the settlement people to join his family for a barn dance. The boys played banjos, fiddle and had a rousing time until near midnight. After all the settlement people had left, Eli broke out Angus' bagpipes and played to the valley, all the old tunes that he knew.

The rustling of Jack cooking awakened Eli from his happy dream. He lay there quietly without opening his eyes for fear of losing the wondrous feeling he was enjoying. He was smiling and had a feeling that he had lost for so long. It was a feeling of love, peace and happiness.

He had a longing for Maggie that he could not put into words. He thought about her for a while longer and opened his eyes.

There *was* a cabin to build for Jack.

CHAPTER FIFTEEN
ROMEOS OF THE VALLEY

As promised, Eli was at the cabin site working as the sun came up. Jack and the "turncoat" Dawg had gone to MacAndrews Store for window putty.

Eli walked around the cabin site and marveled at the progress. He thought to himself, that he and Jack would have been a week or more getting this much done.

He was proud of the progress and of his progeny. He thought how a man never really dies if he has youngins' to keep the bloodline going. He was proud too, that they had kept the MacGowan name pure and respected.

It looked to be a good day for cabin buildin' he thought. "A good day indeed," he said aloud.

Eli heard the approaching train of wagons loaded with MacGowans. He stood and admired the sight, a sight that made his heart feel warm.

Unbeknownst to Eli, Jack and Dawg had met the MacGowan wagons about a mile down the creek. They stopped and spoke of the progress and the weather. Jack did his usual circling around before finally saying what he wanted to say.

"I want to thank you boys for helpin' me with the cabin. I want to thank you for helpin' that hard headed old Scot too. He will not ever say so, but I know he is proud of you all, well, that is about it; I had better get to the store so Red can get the winders made."

The MacGowans all smiled and nodded in response, never saying a word and headed the wagon procession towards Jack's cabin.

Jack rolled on to MacAndrews Store as Dawg peeled off to investigate the settlement.

MacAndrews was setting on the porch as Jack rode up to the store. He acknowledged Jack and said "Corntassel will see to your business inside." Jack replied with a nod.

Corntassel was inside behind the counter waiting on a woman. Jack, still being the ladies man, was very attentive to the transaction; mostly to the woman involved in the transaction.

Corntassel took her money and finished filling up her canvas bag with her supplies. He handed the bag to the woman.

Jack reached for the bag and said let me get that for you ma'am." She turned to Jack and smiled and said "Thank you sir, but I can manage."

Jack observed in detail the dark skin, long black hair, black eyes and pretty smile. She is a pretty woman, Jack thought, Cherokee without a doubt.

She realized he was starring at her as she picked up the sack of provisions and walked to the door. Jack rushed to open the door for the pretty woman, and followed behind her. He noticed her shape, and was pleased with what he saw.

She noticed him noticing her too, and didn't change her smiling expression. Jack offered her a hand down the steps of the store and helped her up to the seat of her wagon. He took her bag of supplies and sat it into the wagon; he said, "Nice to meet you."

She smiled her response, snapped the reigns against the horse's rump, and rolled away from the store.

Jack stood and watched the mystery woman roll down the settlement road out of site. MacAndrews clearing his throat snapped Jack from his stare.

Jack turned and stepped back on the porch.

MacAndrews was smiling a big toothy grin that looked like he knew what Jack was thinking.

"She's a purty thing ain't she?" said MacAndrews.

"Yes she is *that* for sure," said Jack.

"She would make a good woman for a man if he was lookin'," said MacAndrews.

John Corntassel stepped from the store onto the porch. He looked at both men, curious about the conversation they were having. MacAndrews said, "John it looks like Mankiller here has takin' a fancy to your sister."

Jack had a stoic look and said nothing in reply to the statement; although he knew it was a fact.

Corntassel said, "My sister is a good woman, shame that the fever took her man. She has not looked at another man since Bob MacWilliams died. The fever took her only son too. Becky has two grown daughters. Both are married and live in Calhoun. "

"I reckon it has taken her a while to get over losin' them two. I look in on her once in a while she's gettin' better. All she used to do is cry and sit in the cabin." Corntassel continued.

Jack went into the store, Corntassel followed behind. Jack said, "I need winder putty for Eli."

Corntassel turned and rummaged through the shelves, sliding cans of this and that and retrieved the putty.

They concluded the transaction and Jack turned to leave but turned back and said, "Do you think your sister would like a drop in from me?"

John said, "Well, I guess she might. I'll mention you, the next time I see her."

Jack said, "Let me have a pound of that horehound candy John." Corntassel bagged up the candy and took Jack's money.

Jack said, "I'll be down here in a day or two." Corntassel smiled and said, "I'll have word for you about Becky by then."

"So her name is Becky," Jack asked. "Yes, Rebecca but we always called her Becky," said Corntassel. "She is my baby sister."

Jack nodded to Corntassel and left the store. He nodded at MacAndrews still propped up in a chair on the porch.

Jack headed back to the cabin site; he looked around for Dawg but didn't see him nearby. He whistled and called his name; still no

Dawg. He rode up the street a ways and found the old mutt having relations with a young female mutt right in front of the church.

Jack laughed at the expression on Dawg's face, locked up in a precarious state, to say the least. Jack waited a few minutes, they broke free from each other, and Dawg trotted over to Jack.

Jack said "and I thought I was a womanizer" and laughed. "Let's go get some work done, since we have finished our work here."

Jack wheeled his horse around and they headed to the cabin site. Jack still chuckled and Dawg looked at him with a look of contentment.

Back at MacAndrews Store, Corntassel joined MacAndrews on the porch. They sat a while chewing and spitting tobacco juice and thinking.

MacAndrews said, "I think Jack has taken a fancy to your sister." John smiled and said, "It looks like it."

"I figure if he is Eli MacGowan's friend he must be a good man," said Corntassel. MacAndrews nodded his agreement.

"Looks like you have takin' to matchmakin' there John" said MacAndrews through a chuckle. "Maybe," said Corntassel, "Becky needs a good man; she is too young and purdy to be alone."

Jack arrived at the cabin site to find the MacGowan machine running smoothly. They were cutting trees, peeling bark, shaping logs, cutting dovetail notches, and building a fireplace.

Although there was still much to do, Jack could see a cabin starting to take shape. Jack smiled and handed the putty to Eli. He took the putty looked at it and walked over to George.

Eli and Jack checked on the progress of work. It met their approval; it was good to see that his grandsons were learning the skills he had passed down to his sons.

He discussed the work to left to do with his sons and left George in charge of the crew of cabin builders.

Jack remembered the horehound candy, fetched the poke, and distributed a stick to each worker. They all smiled, it was a treat not to be had often; they stopped and took time to enjoy the candy.

Eli smiled and took a piece for himself and nodded his thanks.

He and Jack headed for the wood shop in the barn to build windows and doors. Dawg stayed with the builders, Eli figured it was due to the attention that was getting over there.

They set to work on the chestnut wood, sawing, shaving, and mitering the corners. He had to plane, with his shaper, to form the window moldings to receive the panes of glass.

They laid down a bead of putty for the panes, pressed the glass into place and tacked the glass to keep it put. He puttied each window light until one was finished.

It was hard tedious work. Just what Eli loved to do the most; Jack mostly handed tools and held boards. Eli was glad to have his help and his company.

Jack observed, as they finished each window frame, that Eli was building six windows, not two as he had thought was the plan.

He mentioned this to Eli; he only smiled and said, "I think you will need four windows in your cabin and I want to add two more to Maggie's cabin."

He said Maggie's cabin, thought Jack, wondering what was going on in the old Scots head. Well, back to work, Jack thought. The week is still young and there was much to do.

The MacGowans fell into a routine, arriving at daylight leaving just before dark each day. They had the walls almost up; windows, loft doors, front door, and cellar door were in place. The floor was almost finished as was most of the chimney. Next would be framing for the roof, building the loft floor and ladder and putting in the chinking between the logs.

This week had certainly yielded great progress. At this rate, we should finish up in another week, thought Eli.

Jack was constantly in admiration of the work going on with the cabin. He had the big toothless smile showing most of the time. Eli thought he had not seen him this happy in a long while. That was good he thought.

Well, it was Saturday and Eli needed nails for the roof shakes next week, and they were nearly out of tobacco for their pipes too.

Eli asked Jack if he wanted to get the needed supplies from MacAndrews's store, he agreed and took the wagon down to the settlement to procure the items.

Jack entered the store; it was busier than he had seen it in past visits. Jack allowed it was Saturday and the settlement folks were getting their supplies for next week, as was he.

He hung around in the corner waiting for the crowd to thin out and after a good while, the last person left.

Jack eased over to the counter and said, "I need twenty pounds of nails and two pokes of backer."

Corntassel retrieved and weighed the nails as MacAndrews fetched the tobacco for Jack.

Jack paid for the nails and tobacco and went to the wagon. Corntassel was slowly loading the nails, waiting for Jack to arrive.

Corntassel said, "She would court you if you were a mind too." Jack smiled and said, "Tell her I *am* a mind to court her."

Corntassel said "she will be at church in the mornin' if you want, you can meet her there."

Jack thought long and hard about sittin' in church but allowed it would be worth it to meet Becky. Jack said, "Tell her I'll see her tomorrow at church."

Corntassel said, "No offense but you might want to take a bath and warsh your clothes. We have soap in the store if you want."

Jack smiled and said, "I reckon I must smell purdy gamey and these breeches ain't been warshed in a year or so. They can stand up at night when I pull 'em off. Soap, you say, guess I'll take some."

Corntassel said, "It is three bits;" Jack gave him the coins and he retrieved the soap and handed it to him.

Jack sniffed the bar and said, "It smells a heap better that the lye soap Eli has at the cabin." Jack smiled and said, "It will smooth the waters with Becky, if you show, smellin' good." Jack smiled his agreement, put the soap in his poke and headed back to the cabin.

He met the MacGowans on his return trip. George spoke and said, "We are headin' back early today. Its Saturday, got baths to take, tomorrow is church day." Talk of a bath caused a sense of dread to drown Jack's thoughts. "He said yep bath night, I forgot."

"George said come and join us at church and we'll eat Sunday dinner afterwards at my place. We will have plenty; I think Paw might even come, he never said for sure though."

Jack said, "I'll be there, meetin' Becky MacWilliams."

George and the others showed a big MacGowan grin that he had seen on Eli a thousand times. Jack sensed that they were pleased and surprised at the same time.

Feeling a bit uncomfortable with the spot he was in; Jack said, "I better get going, don't want you boys to miss out of your baths." They all smiled and left for their destinations, which *would* include a bath for all. Jack shuddered at the thought.

Jack arrived at the barn and unhitched the wagon. He rubbed down the mule and fed him.

Eli was finishing a window and said, "I'll be on up to the cabin after feeding and milking."

Jack said, "I'm goin' to church in the mornin'."

Eli said, "I'm thinkin' about it myself and dinner at the George's place after church."

"I guess I can endure the gawkin' by the whole settlement when I walk in to church," Eli said.

Jack said, "I am goin' to set with Becky MacWilliams tomorrow and the boys invited us to dinner too. I reckon I'll take 'em up on the offer."

Eli showed an identical grin to the one the boys had cast at him earlier on the road. "Becky MacWilliams" said Eli; "a good woman there Jack, ain't she a bit young for your old carcass?"

"How old do you think?" said Jack. "I would say about thirty five, maybe forty," said Eli.

Counting on his fingers "Hmmm" said Jack that is only 'bout twenty years difference".

Eli smiled and "said more like thirty years, but that ain't uncommon; she *would* make a good wife."

"Wife," questioned Jack; "I ain't even set next to her yet Eli, just let's see what happens."

"You got a tub Eli?" asked Jack. "A tub for what?" replied Eli. "Well, I reckon we will have to warsh our stinkin' carcasses before courtin' and church," said Jack.

Eli laughed and said, "It is up in the loft," as he pointed up to the next level in the barn, "I'll fetch it."

Jack filled the tub with boiling water, tempered it with a little cool spring water, and slid his wrinkled old body into the water.

Eli saw the bar of soap and asked, "What is this Jack, my soap ain't good enough to scrub that crusty old hide of yours?"

Jack said "it smells like flowers or somethin', Corntassel said it would help take the stink off me."

Eli said, "I still don't see what is wrong with my lye soap;" then he answered his own question with a laugh.

Dawg stood off in the far corner of the cabin, observing the filling of the tub, he remembered the one bath Gussie had given him as a pup and lit out. There was no invitation to the bathing, given Dawg, but he didn't want to take the chance.

They must have used a hundred gallons of water washing their dirty hides and old clothes. They both put on clean nightshirts and ate supper smelling like lilac in springtime.

They heard Dawg return to the porch. Eli opened the door and he came in. Eli gave him his supper and he lay down with a contented look.

Jack told Eli, "You have yourself a regular Romeo there in that old mutt. I caught him romancin' a young bitch in the settlement." They laughed. Dawg looked disgusted and violated; he went back to the porch for the night.

Jack said, "I wish I had some better duds to wear to church in the mornin'. My old buckskins are not much for makin' the ladies take notice."

Eli went into the bedroom and dug through the big chest, found what he was looking for and returned to the front room. Eli handed Jack a suit of clothes and said, "Try these on Jack, for fit."

Jack looked puzzled and Eli said, "They belonged to my Paw. He had two sets; we buried him in the other. All of the boys were too big to wear them so Maw and Maggie kept 'em in the loft."

Jack tried on the pants, shirt, and coat and they fit close enough to wear. He tried on the shoes, smiled, and said, "I look like the preacher in these white men's clothes."

Eli said, "You *will* make Becky's heart pitter pat for sure," they both laughed.

Eli noticed a change in Jack's expression, he knew something big was about to be said. Jack paused for a good while, thinking about the right way to say what was on his mind.

Eli, tired of waiting said, "Jack, just *say* what's on your mind."

Jack looked away and spoke, "Eli, I am too old to be thinkin' about a woman as fine as Becky MacWilliams. What is in this for her? I am an old wore out Cherokee. Ain't got no money, no land, sure ain't got no looks."

Eli laughed and added, "Ain't got no teeth either."

They both laughed, which broke the tension for a bit, then Eli turned serious again, and said, "Jack Mankiller, you are a good man, you are steady, and when you settle down, you will settle down. I never thought you would ever settle down, but you are, and you will be a good provider and maybe even a good father. I think Becky could do worse than to have you. So do not doubt who you are, Jack, she must see something in you she likes, just let it run its course. "

"Well, I reckon that was some straight talk, Eli. I think I do not want to grow old by myself, you have Maggie to take care of you." Jack paused and looked to see the expression on Eli's face. It was a look of sadness.

Jack continued, "Eli, I am meddlin' with your dealins' about Maggie, but ain't you been sick about this long enough, my friend?"

Eli stared off through the open door and didn't reply.

Jack only shook his head in dismay at Eli's hard head.

Eli stood, walked to the door, and closed it and placed the latch in its place. Turned back to Jack and said, "It's been a long day Jack, think I'll turn in for the day.

It *had* been a tiring day, so they went to sleep.

CHAPTER SIXTEEN
THE OLD SCOTS LEAVE THE VALLEY

Eli's sleep was a welcome relief to his tired body. He was ten again and with his grandfather Angus MacGowan. Sitting on the porch, Angus was teaching Eli to play the bagpipes; or the great pipes, as Angus called them.

Angus told him the story of the pipes. It was a sad story Eli thought. He told him about how, in Scotland, each clan had a piper. His duty was to pipe for deaths, births, weddings, and special times.

In his thick Scottish accent, Angus said, "The pipes could stir the Scots in battle, so much, that the English forbid their use. This bagpipe belonged to me seanair," he paused and corrected his Gaelic to English, "me grandfather. Eli, it will be placed in your hands once mastered, before my death."

Eli would not allow himself to think of a world without Angus MacGowan. He was amazing, in Eli's eyes and most everyone else that knew him, for that matter.

As Angus carefully explained the parts of this contraption, Eli marveled at his grandfather's talent when playing the pipes, so he paid close attention to the old man's words. Angus explained the parts of the bagpipes, pointed to the bag; "This is made from leather, and these are the five pipes, the blowpipe, the bass, the tenors, and the chanter. The chanter makes the notes", as he pointed out the eight holes for his fingers.

Angus spent hours and hours working with Eli. He knew he would be *the* one, to learn. He showed interest from the earliest time Angus could remember. He thought Eli was a true Scot, through and through.

Eli thought it was more than he could learn, but he would not give up. He and Angus spent hours practicing. The sound emanating from Eli's practice sessions hurt everyone's ears that were close enough to hear the lessons.

Sarah MacGowan dreaded Eli's practice time but said nothing that would discourage her young son. The sessions on rainy days were especially dreadful. She knew the pipes could not be out in the rain due to fear of warping, which would be the end of it.

Angus had spare parts made but he hoped not to use them. Pipes took years to let the wood season before drilling and Angus had informed all in the MacGowan clan of this fact many times. The bagpipes commanded great respect and near reverence in the household.

Eli's practice finally showed fruit. He played for the family and Angus often and all could hear the progress. Five years into the teaching, Angus told Eli there was nothing else he could teach; he was now the master of the pipes.

Eli beamed with Scottish pride. He visited Angus often and played for him. Angus became too old to have the wind to play and knew his days were short, on this land.

One day, as Eli had finished playing for his grandfather and started to leave, handing the pipes to Angus.

Angus refused, and said the bittersweet words that Eli never forgot. Angus said, "Eli, me son, I am ready to turn the pipes over to you. I dunno have the wind and canno teach you anythin' new, so take these pipes and hold them with respect. Give them to a grandson that will respect and learn the art."

Eli looked puzzled and saw Granny Gullie's eyes fill with tears; they both knew what Angus was saying.

Eli stood tall and looked Angus MacGowan, straight in the eyes, and although blurred with tears, he could see what a special moment this was in his life.

It was not just receiving the bagpipes of four generations of MacGowans. The transfer of these pipes that had endured the journey from Dalwhinnie in the Highlands of Scotland to America meant it was a changing of traditions, from one generation to Eli's generation. This moment was a beginning, and an end.

Eli reverently said, "Angus MacGowan, from this day to my last breath, I vow to keep the traditions of the pipes, and to keep the stories alive; to give to that grandson that is worthy to carry it forward. I love you grandpa, I always will." Eli's voice cracked, as he was finished.

Angus said nothing, only smiled and nodded his response. Turned and slowly shuffled into the cabin, never to see his beloved pipes again.

Angus MacGowan died on a cold winter afternoon, with four of his sons, two daughters, and his always-loving Gullie by his side.

Eli sat on the porch in the cold and listened to his Granny Gullie crying for her husband, and felt Angus' spirit float away from the Watauga Valley.

Eli imagined that Angus hovered above the valley for a while to say goodbye, then sailed across the dark Atlantic to his beloved Scotland, the land of his birth.

He would say goodbye to his brothers and sisters there and join the old Scots in heaven. That is how Eli painted Angus' death in his mind; it made it easier for him to accept.

It was a hard time.

Angus was the patriarch of the MacGowans, the original interloper of the clan to enter the Watauga Valley; as well as the first to live in America.

He *would* leave his mark on this land as could be witnessed by the children, grandchildren, and great grandchildren that were scattered across this new land.

Eli went to the hill that overlooked the MacGowan farm took out his pipes and played all the tunes his grandfather had taught him. He cried, as he played the sad sounding melodies that filled the valley. All who heard would know that Angus had passed.

Gullie listened as she prepared her husband's body for the grave. She talked to Angus' body as his spirit was out there listening to Eli playing. "Angus do you hear Eli, I know you can, and I know how proud you must be, I can see that wee smile, you sweet old Scot." This somehow made her task easier.

She washed his body, dressed him in his best clothes, folded his arms and combed his hair; this was the last thing she could do for Angus in this life. She leaned over, kissed him, and whispered." I'll see you in heaven, my sweet Angus."

William and his brothers placed their father's corpse into the coffin and placed nickels on his eyes to keep them closed. The pall was set in the cabin for the wake that would come later.

Eli could see the hundreds of people who walked and rode in the cold night to participate in the wake for Angus MacGowan. Eli had never seen a sight like this, there was food and drink, tears and laughter.

The men who knew Angus told of his good deeds as well as his misdeeds in life. They told of a man that was hard working and a bit rambunctious too.

Eli would miss his grandfather but knew this was the way of things in the valley. You are born, you live your life and you go into the ground and on to heaven.

Angus always said he hoped to leave nothing but a good name and take nothing but a pure soul to the next life. Eli thought his grandfather had accomplished both.

William MacGowan said, "It is a sad day for this valley and this family, we shall have hard work, to match the standard our father, Angus MacGowan has set." Gullie said, "Angus has left his good name in good hands, my sons and daughters."

They buried Angus on top of the hill where he had laid the bodies of his four young children. It was the MacGowan Cemetery, from that day forward.

Gullie shortly followed the path that Angus had blazed before her. She just simply lost any will to live and Eli watched her wither away. She was just not whole without Angus and she could not find anything, to fill the void left by his passing.

Eli thought about his last conversation with his Granny Gullie. She could barely speak above a whisper, but it was a good talk.

From her bed, she softly said, "Eli I expect you to be a good man, like William and Angus. Be a good Scot, be fair in all your dealin', never lie to or cheat anyone. Stand up and speak your mind when necessary, keep your peace, when it is the proper thing to do.

If you make whisky to sell, sip only do not drink it son, it will take your soul. Spit in the devil's eye every chance you get and above all, fear The Almighty and try to follow the commandments."

Eli burned her every word into his mind forever. He loved his Granny Gullie and thought she was a wise woman. The conversation waned. She said she needed, now to rest for a while.

Eli tucked her in tight and kissed her forehead; she smiled a wee smile at him and winked. He had seen that wink a thousand times. That same wink she displayed as she slipped the last biscuit to him under the table or placed a piece of candy in his hand unexpectedly, or maybe after she had put her twist on happenings, that kept him from getting his hide tanned by his father.

That was the last time she would wink or smile at Eli.

They found Gillian MacGowan, the next morning, with a peaceful look, lying in her bed with Eli's tuck still in place.

There were tears from all, but mostly tears of joy that she was with Angus and happy now.

They placed her between Angus and her four children. Eli played the pipes and cried for his Granny Gullie.

It *was* a hard time.

Eli woke from his sleep, with tears on his face and his bed. He could see the early signs of a new day through the solitary window of the cabin.

He still had the words of the old folks circling in his mind. "Fear the Almighty and follow the commandments," Granny Gullie said. They would not leave his head, so he rose from bed and walked to the porch.

Eli repeatedly heard Gullie's words. Eli yelled, "***Enough now!***" He pointed to the heavens and said, "You are not fightin' fair bringin' my dead granny into this fray!"

Jack dashed onto the porch in his nightshirt to see what the commotion was. He asked are, "Eli, who are you hollerin' at?"

Eli said, "Oh, just a contest between me and The Almighty." Jack grinned and said, "Oh, *that's* all."

He patted Eli on the shoulder and said, "Let's get some breakfast; we have got a big day today, church, courtin' and eatin' to follow."

CHAPTER SEVENTEEN
WHAT A DAY THIS HAS BEEN

Jack noticed Eli was not in the cabin while he was shaving for church. He walked to the door and looked out on the porch. There stood Eli with scissors in hand trimming his beard. Eli noticed Jack and asked if he would trim his hair. Jack said, "I will as soon as I'm finished shavin'."

Jack wondered about Eli, he seemed very quiet this morning. Must have a lot on his mind Jack thought.

Jack finished up with shaving and trimmed Eli's white hair. "I think that will pass," said Jack. "Good enough then," said Eli, "I better finish gettin' ready so we can head to the settlement. Don't want to be late, do we?"

Eli finished up, hitched up the horses to the wagon, and headed toward the settlement. Dawg didn't join the two fashionable looking gentlemen. "Dawg must be worn out from all the excitement of the week, he *is* old," said Jack. Eli nodded his agreement and they rolled on to the church. They hitched up the wagon and strolled up to the church.

A goodly and, for the most part, godly crowd, was already at the church when Eli and Jack arrived. Both men had enough apprehension to fill a washtub, but proceeded to the door of the church anyway.

Pastor Emmons was on guard at the front door. Eli had not spoken to him for years and the last words he had were not too godly. The pastor reached out his hand and said good to see you again Brother MacGowan. Eli only nodded and said, "Don't make too much out of this." Pastor Emmons smiled and patted Eli on the back, and said, "Welcome my friend, welcome."

Jack failed at his attempt to skirt around Eli and the pastor, but could not escape, just as he entered the door, Pastor Emmons said. "I don't think I have had the pleasure sir." Jack said, "I am Jack Mankiller, from Washington County, Eli's friend."

Pastor Emmons said, "Well, if you are Eli's friend you must be a good man, welcome to our church. Enjoy the services." Jack grinned, revealing to the pastor his lack of a full set of teeth and proceeded into the house of the Lord.

Eli had found his sons in the church and noticed the side of the MacGowan pew where he and Maggie had always, sat was unoccupied. Eli sat in his usual spot, as he had for all the years before, as if nothing had transpired to the contrary, between him and God. Eli could feel the stares from the congregation but just ignored the sensation and set his jaw to get this over.

Jack had fared much better, he sauntered over to where Becky MacWilliams was sitting and she looked up at him and smiled. Eli thought Jack was going to melt on the spot. She slid over and he parked his rump on the end of the pew beside her. They acted stiff towards each other, but both thought it was nice to be this close.

The singing started; everyone who could remember Eli knew how fine his baritone voice sounded in the congregation. Eli was not in a singing mood today. It was going to be a long morning for him, he thought.

Jack thought it was going to be a good morning, sitting next to this fine looking Becky MacWilliams.

Neither Jack nor Eli paid much attention to the sermon. Jack had his mind on Becky; Eli's mind was on Maggie.

While Pastor Emmons offered the closing prayer, Eli took the opportunity to slip out of the church to avoid the parting glances and glad-handing, during his exit.

He was waiting by his son George's wagon, when Jack and Becky strolled out of the church. Eli said hello to Becky and told Jack they could take the wagon, he would ride with George.

Jack grinned and thanked Eli. Becky smiled and Jack hoisted her onto the wagon seat for the ride to George MacGowans for Sunday dinner.

Eli sat with George and his wife, who were holding their granddaughter little Maggie. She handed her to Eli; he again melted at the sight of this miniature version of *his* Maggie.

The trip to Georges seemed to pass quickly; his grandsons sat by Eli and questioned him about hunting and fishing, important talk to young men. The boys were happy to have their grandpa back again. Eli thought it was good too.

They ate under the big chestnut at George's cabin. It was obvious that George had used Eli's table as a pattern for his. He thought that was the MacGowan way. Pass all the good in life on to the next generation.

They all ate their fills and talked and laughed. The children played in the branch. Jack and Becky made eyes at each other the whole time of the dinner. It was near sickening to see, thought Eli.

Jack had the hook set on him already by the widow MacWilliams, or at least it sure looked that way to Eli. That would be good for Jack and Becky they both needed someone. Someone like Maggie, Eli thought.

Well, the boys broke out the fiddles and banjos and started playing up a storm. Eli jumped in, played the fiddle, and danced a reel on the porch. The youngins' were amazed that this old man could still move like that. Jack jumped in and danced a few rounds with Becky.

The afternoon passed too quickly for all. Soon it was time to load up the wagon and head back to the cabin. Eli rode on the back of the wagon so Becky and Jack could hug up on the wagon seat, all the way to Becky's cabin.

They smooched on the porch for a while, and Jack finally let her break away. They talked for a while and Jack pointed to Eli to inform Becky of his impatient traveling companion, smooched one last time, and strutted to the wagon.

Eli said, "Looks like you are about to start crowin' there old man." Jack only smiled and hopped up on the wagon seat and gave Becky a last glance, she was standing on the porch waving, as the wagon rolled away.

Jack and Eli pulled the wagon into the barn and tied the horses. Jack said we had better get our work clothes on. Eli nodded and said, "Yes have to feed and milk, do not want to get our Sunday duds dirty."

They closed the barn door and Jack said, "What was that?" Eli stood and listened to the sound coming from the side of the barn. They walked to the side and there lay Dawg. They walked to Dawg and saw that he had dead rattlesnake in the grip of his jaws. Dawg was laying there whimpering and had a sad look in his eyes.

Eli and Jack figured the worse. Jack said, "That rattler has got him on the neck, Eli", as he pried the dog's jaws apart and removed the huge dead rattlesnake. Eli investigated the bite and knew they would have to get to work if Dawg would have a chance of survival. He knew it was unlikely that Dawg would make it, but he was bound to try.

Dawg whimpered as Eli picked the dirty old mutt up in his Sunday suit and carried him toward the branch. He had learned from observing snake bit animals as they went to the cool water. He didn't know why but he placed Dawg into the cool water and cradled his head.

Jack said, "We need to bleed that bite Eli," and he proceeded to cut a slice across the two puncture holes in the dog's neck. Jack squeezed the poison out with the blood. Eli just talked to Dawg and tried to comfort him. Dawg looked at Jack and Eli with trusting eyes; he knew that what they were doing was for his good.

Eli said, "You hang on Dawg, don't you die on me," as he stroked his head. Dawg only looked with sadness in his eyes and started to fade away. The last words he would hear, in this life, were words of love, from Eli and Jack.

The next sight Dawg saw was young Gussie laughing and motioning him to come and play. He took off and ran to him with a young dog's legs, not the old worn out legs he left with the dead body Eli was cradling, in the branch.

Eli said with a cracking voice, "he's gone Jack; Dawg is dead."

Jack stood as if the wind had gone out of his sail, not knowing what to say to his friend; a man that had endured too much pain to endure one more drop. This was more than a drop; to Eli this was a river. Eli stood and laid Dawg on the bank of the branch.

Both men stared at this big hairy beast of a dog. He was a friend to all, a hunter, a guard and a protector.

Jack broke the silence and said, "Eli you know that rattler could have got one of the horses or maybe one of us; Dawg might have kept us from bein' rattler bit." Eli said, "at least he died for somethin' not just a wasted life; guess we need to put him in the ground. I'll get somethin' to cover him up."

Jack said, "Let me change and I'll bury him for you Eli."

Eli said, "Good, I've dug enough graves to suit me for a long while; I'll change and do the chores."

Jack laid Dawg by the branch near the old chestnut tree. He thought it was a nice spot. He had often seen Dawg cooling there on sunny days and knew he would like this place.

Eli joined Jack as he placed a stone at the head of Dawg's grave. Eli asked, "Reckon critters go to heaven?" Jack said I reckon so, "It would not be much of a heaven without good huntin' dogs up there."

Eli said, "I reckon Dawg is at peace then."

That was all of the talk about Dawg, this day.

Jack said, "That rattler is as long as you Eli; I'm gonna skin him out will make some good belts."

Jack went to skinning the rattlesnake while Eli fixed a little supper. The combination of the stuffing that took place at George's place after church and the loss of old Dawg, left both men with a small appetite.

They drank some coffee, puffed on the pipe for a good while, not much conversation, just lots of thinking.

Jack was thinking about Dawg and Becky; Eli about Dawg and Maggie; some serious thinking for sure.

Tomorrow would be a workday. Eli hoped hard work would keep his mind off Maggie and Dawg.

"What a day this has been," said Eli. They turned in for the day; hoping for peaceful dreams.

CHAPTER EIGHTEEN
IT'S OVER NOW

The next day, the boys arrived on schedule and joined Eli and Jack. They asked about Dawg and Eli told them the sad news. Jack told the work crew about how big the rattler was and showed them the skinned out hide nailed to the side of the barn. Eli thought this might not be the best thing to talk about since they would be working within a stone's throw from the spot the rattlesnake had met its end by the jaws of Dawg. The entire work party spent the morning with snakes on their minds. They were a bit jumpy at strange sounds and movements. That was forgotten when dinner arrived.

Eli noticed that the MacGowan women had picked up Becky on the way; she would be their guest for dinner. Eli thought there was definitely some matchmakin' going on here.

Jack Mankiller perked up, went to the spring branch, and washed up his face and hands. Eli joined him and could not pass up the opportunity to poke fun at his friend. "That woman has you tore up Mankiller," said Eli. Jack only grinned and replied, "I ain't felt like this about a woman in years, Eli. Can't say exactly what this feelin' is, but it is good."

Eli looked serious and said, "All jokin' aside Jack, you need you a good woman and she fits that bill for sure." Jack smiled and said, "Glad you approve Red; I'm gonna go after her like a fox after a hen. If she will have me, I aim to marry her." "Whoa there Jack, you've only knowed her for a week. Maybe give it a month or two anyway," Eli, said chuckling. "Nope," said Jack, "knowed it when I first met Becky Walker, know it now with Becky MacWilliams. I aim to finally marry me a Becky, if she will have me."

Eli looked serious and said, "you know Jack, when I first laid eyes on my Maggie, I knowed she would be mine and she told me she felt the same about me. It was that day they rolled into the valley and stopped to talk to my Paw."

Eli looked sad, Jack knew what he was thinking and felt bad about causing this pain for his friend.

"Well, we better eat," said Jack.

"You better get down there to Becky MacWilliams before she gets tard of waitin'." Jack smiled and they headed to the dinner table under the big chestnut.

Jack goo gooed at Becky more than he ate and then they walked off, holding hands. Every eye at the table watched and every face had a big grin across it. Except for little Maggie who was busy throwing beans across the table and giggling. Eli walked around the table, picked her up, sat, and fed her off his plate. He made sure she had an ample supply of beans to throw too.

Eli was amazed at the resemblance that this little Maggie had to *his* Maggie. It gave Jack a peaceful feeling holding his great granddaughter; she liked his company too and rubbed green beans through his white hair. Eli didn't care; she would do as she pleased around him.

The boys finished and headed back to work as Eli and little Maggie sat and enjoyed each other, oblivious to the goings on around them.

The women had cleared the table and loaded the wagon; little Maggie's mother came to take her from Eli, but she didn't have the heart and sat beside him and little Maggie.

Her name was Annie, the young wife of George's son Andrew. Eli had only had short conversations with the young mother but he liked her from the start. Not just because she was the sweet mother of little Maggie but there was just something special in her manner that Eli thought made her a cut above.

She said," Mister MacGowan, I know we hardly know each other, but I want to talk to you from my heart."

Eli turned and said, "I am listenin' missy."

She spoke, in a soft sweet voice, "I have prayed for you every night. I have prayed that you and Misses MacGowan would make peace and make this family whole again."

Eli thought these words sounded too wise to come from her young mouth but he continued to listen.

She said, "I pray every night that you will make peace with God and Maggie." Her eyes welled with tears, "I lost a baby to the fever too, and it was hard and nearly killed me. I could not blame the Lord; he was what got me through that hard time. I still have days where I just have to go off somewhere and have a good cryin' spell. So I can't dream of what you and Maggie went through losin' three youngins'."

Eli wondered if the All Mighty had sent this angel to give him one more chance. He put his arm around her and started to cry. It was a hard shaking cry where you let it all out. He was broken; the hard stone that had encased his heart was shattered into dust. Eli felt that old warmth in his body, the warmth that had left him on that cold rainy day when he laid his son in the ground.

Little Maggie sat and watched in silence. Her young mother and this old man must have been a sight to her little blue eyes. Eli cried and Annie hugged him and cried until they had attracted the attention of all the MacGowans within earshot.

The women came first and joined with the crying, some started to pray for Eli. His sons followed shortly, George, Robert, Timothy, and Thomas MacGowan. They wrapped their burly arms around their father and cried with him, and then they all dropped to their knees and prayed loud enough that the settlement folk surely could hear them. This lasted well over an hour, praying, crying, and embracing. Annie MacGowan had broken the spell.

Eli stood, raised his arms towards heaven, and softly spoke to the sky, "It's over now Lord".

Eli felt good again; he was smiling and happy again. He had found himself. He knew The Almighty placed Annie in his path, to be a guide, and she was an angel to Eli, he would always hold a special room in his heart for her.

The hugging lasted a good while, as he hugged the last grandson, Becky MacWilliams came up and hugged Eli and said, "Bless your heart, Eli MacGowan, I have prayed for this day for years, our prayers have been answered."

Then there was Jack; trying to hide behind a chestnut tree, Eli walked over to him and said, "I have found my way again, my friend."

Jack said with a quiver in his old throat, "I had hoped you would Eli. You have been on the wrong trail a good while now. I have been sending word up to the Lord for you, since the day he sent me here. I do not know how to pray, that good, or maybe I do, all I know is that it has worked. I hope someday the Lord will show me the way, like he has you. I am starting to see good signs that He may have already started, we shall see, Eli. All I know is that it is good to have the whole Eli MacGowan back again."

Eli said, "I thank you for coming, I know now that nothing happens by chance, you were sent to me to help me find the right path. My brother, Jack, I have prayed for you too, not so much in recent years, due to my standing with The Almighty, but I guess you are an answer to somebody's prayers, for me."

Eli turned his attention to all the MacGowans in front of him. "The Almighty has sent me Jack Mankiller, the best tracker in this land, to help me find my way. His comin' has led to this cabin, this cabin was the reason you are all here today. This was the All Mighty's doin'."

Eli looked to the heavens, and said, "Thank you for not givin' up on me Lord."

He looked at Jack and said, "I am not whole yet." Jack grinned and knew what Eli was thinking.

"I must go somewhere Jack, stay and keep things goin'; I'll be back tomorrow." Jack nodded a yes, because he could not speak, due to the boulder in his throat.

Eli walked to his wagon, emptied the contents onto George's wagon, climbed up on the seat. He paused and thought. Down in Calhoun, sweet Maggie MacGowan was awaiting him, while little Maggie MacGowan was behind him, with her sweet mother, Annie. Eli thought how things in life come full circle. The Lord had sent Maggie to be his wife and that union resulted in the life of little Maggie, to complete the circle.

Eli smiled, snapped the reins on the mule's rumps and turned toward Calhoun, where the other half of him, that would make him whole, would be waiting.

Half a day's ride down the Hiwassee River, Maggie spent her days with her firstborn son Isaac, and his wife Rachel. Most of their children had grown up, married, and lived elsewhere.

Maggie and Rachel had become friends. They ran the store sometimes, while Isaac visited the "boys" in Washington County, who ran his other two general stores.

Maggie and Rachel had learned they could get along without a man, but neither particularly liked being away from their husbands.

Maggie knew she was welcome at Isaac and Rachel's home, but longed for Eli MacGowan, and her cabin on MacGowan Creek. She had been so happy there, until the fever took so much of her happiness from her. She had cried many days and nights in Calhoun but still managed to keep her happy manner about her.

Everyone in the Calhoun Church adored and admired her. They saw Maggie as an example of determination and faith.

This day she was busy stocking dry goods with Isaac and Rachel. Once the stocking was completed she retired to the porch, sat, and watched the Hiwassee River rolling on its journey to the Tennessee River, only a few miles downstream. It was a peaceful sight and helped her to think.

Her thoughts today were on Eli. A strong feeling was on her heart today, a feeling that a big change was coming. Tears were streaming down her face as Rachel joined her on the porch. Rachel saw the tears on Maggie's face and knew she was thinking about Eli. Rachel said, "A slow day today Mom," as she called Maggie, "want to take a walk on the river." "No, not today honey, maybe tomorrow," Maggie said. Rachel nodded and sat by Maggie.

They sat and rocked for a while and watched the wagons, horses, and people walking up and down Main Street. They made small talk and Maggie said, "I guess I better make supper." Rachel said, "no, sit I'll fix it Mom."

Maggie stayed and rocked. She thought about her boys and grandbabies up the river and over the mountains. She wished she could wrap her arms around them all. Not knowing about them was worrisome to her and she tried to think that they were all fine, but she *still* worried. She *was* a mother after all.

Maggie sat and rocked, thinking for a good while.

Rachel said, "Mom, supper is ready."

Maggie, somewhat surprised that time had passed that quickly, rose and gave one last look up Main Street, as she always did. Just in case one of her youngins' might be coming or even maybe Eli MacGowan. She was starting to worry that she might never see Eli come down the street. She knew how hard headed that old Scot was, but she had not given up completely and never would. She prayed for him every day, and knew that The Lord worked in His time, not hers.

Although it was getting dusky dark and it was hard to see, and with her eyes, not being what they used to be; that man in the wagon coming down Main Street sure looked a lot like Eli MacGowan. No, she thought, not tonight, her heart sank and she rose to go into the store for supper. Something told her to look again as the wagon stopped in front of the MacGowan General Store.

She saw those blue eyes peering from a face framed by white hair. Her heart raced and she grabbed the porch railing to keep from tumbling into the street.

Eli looked sheepishly at Maggie, would she take him back or ask him to leave. He had been such a dern fool, he thought. It would be fair enough if she chunked rocks at me, he thought.

Seconds slowed to minutes as they stood and looked at each other. He saw the little red-faced girl of fourteen that day in the back of her Pa's wagon.

Maggie saw the lanky, bashful, red haired boy looking at her across from William MacGowan's table, under the old shade tree.

Maggie smiled and said, "Eli, Eli MacGowan, is that you?" Eli smiled and said, "Yes Maggie MacGowan, it's what's left of me."

Eli climbed down and walked up the first step, Maggie stopped his advance by jumping and wrapping her arms around Eli's neck. Maggie cried and screamed. Eli only grinned and hugged her, with tears running down his face.

Eli said, "Maggie, I have been such a hard headed mule, please forgive me." Maggie said, "There is nothin' that needs to be said, it's good to have you back again Eli MacGowan. I have missed you for so long, you old fool."

Isaac and Rachel, and for that matter half of Calhoun, had heard the entire commotion. Isaac stood in the door, Rachel stood behind him, wrapped her arms around his waist and laid her head on his back and started to sob.

Eli carried Maggie up onto the porch, where Isaac and Rachel joined in on the hugging. It lasted a good while; the town people observed, most knew what was going on and smiled their approval.

Isaac said, "Good to see you again Paw, real good." Rachel hugged Eli, she had always loved this old man, he was someone she respected and the feeling was mutual.

Eli said, "It is good to be back son. I love you and Rachel, so much."

Rachel said, "Come in Paw, supper is on the table."

Eli smiled; the welcome by Isaac and Rachel was good indeed. He said, "There is somethin' I need to say to Maggie first."

He stood, trying to think of how to say it right; then he just spoke from his heart. "Maggie, Isaac, Rachel, I have been a fool for these years; I have said and done things that I regret." Eli continued, "I have been at war with the All Mighty Himself, I have been at war with myself; hatred and bitterness has ruled my life. I know that I am to blame, no one else, and ask that you all will forgive my foolish deeds and words."

"I want to ask you all to let me back into your lives."

"I want Maggie to come home."

They hugged and all said they loved him, and forgave him. Isaac thought he had been a hardheaded mule, but he understood, having a large portion of Eli MacGowan's blood, in his veins too.

Maggie said, "Help me load my things and we will get started home." Eli laughed, "I thought we would stay here if Isaac will let us, and we can get started at first light."

Rachel said, "Of course you are always welcome here Eli, come let's eat and talk."

Eli felt like a mountain crumbled from his old shoulders, and he felt completely happy, for the first time in years. It was a good feeling.

He hugged and kissed Maggie all the way to the supper table. The meal was good, because Rachel was a good cook, but it was eating with Maggie, that seasoned the food to perfection.

That big toothy grin didn't leave Eli's weathered old face, even as he slept. There was Maggie by his side, and it was not a dream this time.

It was a *very* good time!

CHAPTER NINETEEN
MADE WHOLE AGAIN

Eli woke from the sweetest night's rest he could remember. There lay Maggie, her sweet head on his shoulder. It was just as he remembered back at the cabin when things were right with the world. He listened to her breathing. He could hear through the open window, the people starting to mill around in the town.

He thought how good it would be to have Maggie back at the cabin. What they could still do with their lives, how they could have some fun mixed in with hard work. He was ready to get started, but didn't want to wake Maggie.

Maggie opened her smiling eyes and cooed, "Mornin' Elijah MacGowan." It sounded sweet to his ears; he had missed this all those mornings since they had parted ways.

He said, "Mornin' Maggie MacGowan, look who's here." She smiled and said, "It's about time." She pecked him on the cheek as he hugged her tight.

They heard Rachel in the kitchen starting breakfast. Maggie said, "I had better go help," Eli said, "Lay still, she will be fine by herself; lay here with me Maggie, let me be sure this is real, and not a dream." She poked him in the ribs and made him jump and laugh. "It's not a dream MacGowan. You had better get used to me, because I am never going away again, you hear me," said Maggie.

"I hear, I hear, stop pokin' my ribs," he laughed. They wrestled around for a while like two children. He kissed her and said, "Let's get goin' Maggie; I've got a cabin to finish."

"A cabin" Maggie inquired. "Yes, the boys and me are buildin' a cabin for Jack Mankiller and maybe his new wife."

Maggie jumped up, propped her elbows on Eli chest, and said, "Jack Mankiller is gettin' *married?*"

"Well, maybe I said, him and Becky MacWilliams are courtin' and sparkin' purdy heavy. Jack talks like he's gonna marry her, if she will have him," said Eli.

Maggie's mouth gaped open in amazement at the news. "Jack and Becky, that's a good match, about time that old Indian is settlin' down and Becky needs a good man but ain't Jack a little old for her? I guess not," she said, answering her own question.

"Well, that is good news Eli. You know Jack stopped by here in the winter, he was headed to Georgia, but said he would stop and look in on you on the way."

Eli smiled, "He looked in all right, moved in is more like it; I was glad to see him and glad he's stayin', he's been good company for me, helped me in a lot of ways."

"I thought he would," a grinning Maggie said, "I thought he would."

Eli figured he would not hear the whole story, but he figured Maggie and Jack were in cahoots about his visit. It didn't matter to Eli, things worked out to the good, he thought.

"Let's get some breakfast," Eli said, "I'm starvin'," Maggie only laughed, "When are you not starvin' Eli MacGowan?"

"I missed your cookin' Maggie, you can see," as he pulled his nightshirt up showing his naked old butt.

Maggie smacked his behind and said, "Get your clothes on you old fool. I'll fill in some of that loose hide, when I get back to cookin' at the cabin." Eli smiled his approval and Maggie smiled at her husband as he pulled on his breeches.

As he pulled his nightshirt, off. She could see the claw marks that the bear had left all those years ago when he and Jack had their run in with the angry critter. She could also see the familiar scars, from knifes and hacking, from Indian War battles.

She thought of how many scars this sweet old man had, most were not visible; they were scars on his heart. She smiled and thought he has survived much, this old Scot that she loved more than the world.

"Are you goin' to wait all day or are you gettin' up for breakfast Maggie?" She knew that patience was a virtue that Eli had not acquired and the she had better get going.

She summarized the day in her head, eat, load the wagon and go home, her home on MacGowan Creek at last. Then, she joined Eli in getting dressed, splashed water on her face and headed downstairs, hand in hand. She thought Eli was holding her hand a little tight, guessed he feared letting her go again. She smiled and thought she was not going anywhere except back to their home, *today!*

They sat and ate a good breakfast with Isaac, Rachel and their two youngest daughters Martha and Susie. Eli picked at them in his usual way that he had with children. He had not seen them for over two years and tried to make up for a lot of lost time.

Conversation was quick and diverse. Many subjects were covered. There was a lot of catching up to do and that they did. Rachel glowed at the talk of her children and grandchildren up in Washington County.

Rachel's talk reminded Eli of what his stubborn ways had cost him; years of time with his family. Years he would never get back. He thought he would have to double up on his time left and try to spend time with all his children. He would have to talk to Maggie about that.

Isaac and Rachel talked about all the progress in the valley. Isaac said, "Paw the railroad is down to Sweetwater and will be comin' to Calhoun next year."

He pointed out the window and said the trestle will cross right over by the big oak by the river." That will make the trip to Knoxville and Jonesborough just a matter of a day. A post can be sent to the boys and back here in a few days, and we plan on taking more trips to see the boys."

A serious cast washed over Eli's face and he pondered what his son had said, then he spoke. "I reckon this country is gettin' too crowded, will be like Knoxville in a few years. If we were younger Maggie, I might just get out of here and head to open land."

Maggie smiled and said, "Eli MacGowan, you have enough land to keep your privacy, and we are too old and to settled here to move."

Eli laughed and said, "Yep, Maggie we will stay put, I'll be in the ground before I'll hear a train whistle tootin' up the Hiwassee and spewin' its blackness and cinders."

Maggie smilingly said, "We have our roots planted in this part of Tennessee now Eli and we need not uproot to keep away from the trains and people."

Eli said, "I reckon you *are* right. I have studied about that and figured you *are* right sometimes."

Maggie's mouth gaped open for a good while, she said nothing, and just tried to be sure she had heard the words, and was not dreaming. "Eli, did you really say you could have been wrong about some things," asked Maggie? "Now don't get carried away Maggie, I just said you are right sometimes, I am still right pert near all the time." Eli said with a smile.

Eli and Maggie were entertaining the young members around the breakfast table and for that matter, Isaac and Rachel too. Maggie realized this and said, "Eli look what a show you are puttin' on in front of Martha and Susie!" Eli only laughed again and said, "It's good for them to see at an early age what a wise grandpa they have."

Maggie smiled and said, "Oh, Eli you are a *sight!*"

They consumed breakfast and the conversation slowed, Maggie took the opportunity to say, "Well, Eli we better get the wagon loaded and head back to the cabin." "I know there is plenty of work waitin' in the cabin, it will take me a month to clean up after you and Jack and you probably have had Dawg in that cabin too."

Eli only laughed and said, "It could use a bit of cleanin' I would say you are right Maggie. That's why I came to get you, as he slapped her on the rump." She feigned a slap to Eli and laughed. It is good to be together he thought, very good indeed.

Eli had a moment of dread slice through his happiness, there *was* the bad news to tell her about Dawg and he knew he would have to tell Maggie. He allowed that would keep for a latter time. He *would* tell her, when the time was right.

They loaded up Maggie's things that she brought as well as the feather bed that Isaac and Rachel had given her.

She promised Martha and Susie that they could come up and stay after school finished up. Their eyes lit up at that word. They would miss their granny.

Rachel hugged Eli and Maggie and with a quivering voice said, "I am goin' to miss you, so much, Maggie MacGowan." Isaac only shook his father's hand, hugged his mother, and walked into the store to prevent anyone from seeing his emotions on display. Maggie and Rachel watched Isaac go into the store and looked at each other and smiled, they both *had* married MacGowans after all.

Eli snapped the reigns and headed the wagon towards MacGowan Creek. It was a typical spring morning in the Hiwassee Valley; the skies were blue, with just a little cool nip in the air. They rolled out of Calhoun and headed up the Hiwassee River towards Columbus. Eli thought the weather was good and the company was even better. It was the same thing Maggie was thinking as she snuggled next to Eli and held to his waist to steady the seating on the bumpy road. Eli beamed as he steered the horses along the road; he waved and said, "Mornin' neighbor" to every wagon and rider he met.

He observed the worn condition of the wagon road. He figured it was from all the too and fro traffic from the settlements to Calhoun.

They stopped in Columbus, near midday, parked the wagon by the river in the shade and ate the bread, meat, and fried apple pies that Rachel had packed for their trip. They could see the ferry from where they parked and they watched as it shuttled wagons and riders back and forth across the Hiwassee. Eli thought it was good entertainment. He could sit and watch for hours, but not today.

Maggie opened up the cloth that covered the fried apple pies and said, "Rachel must have thought we were extra hungry today, she has put a half dozen in here." Eli said, "We could save some for tonight, Jack would surely like one with his evenin' coffee and smoke." Maggie giggled and said, "If a certain Scot does not eat them all on the way." Eli grinned and they packed the dinner provisions and prepared to start the wagon rolling again.

Maggie said, "Must we hurry Eli, let's sit by the river and rest a bit longer." Eli thought, we do not have time to waste here but didn't say it aloud. He thought a bit, smiled at Maggie, and said, "I reckon we have a little while Maggie, let's spread the quilt by the river bank and rest a bit."

Maggie fetched the quilt, grabbed Eli's big paw and pulled him towards the riverbank. They found a nice level spot under a nice oak, spread the quilt, and sat. Maggie laid her head on Eli's big strong arm, they lay, and listened to the rhythmic sound of the river rolling along.

The warm spring sun covered the valley like a blanket, and the tree buds were just about ready to pop. It was one of those days, one when a full belly and the warmth of the sun became the enemy of hard work. Eli often fought the urge to sleep during the day, thinking hard work would keep the sleepiness at bay. Today there was no hard work and Maggie was quickly asleep, Eli soon followed her lead.

Dreams, what a wonderful condition, they take you from one land to another without moving a finger. Eli was going back in time, as was Maggie. Their dreams intertwined on this wonderful spring day. Maggie and Eli were just married and were in their cabin in Watauga. It was a cold winter morning; the sun had not peaked over the mountain. Eli opened the door and saw the snow had piled up against the cabin door during the night.

He had failed to keep the fire stoked and he stirred in the ashes hoping to find an ember or spark to light a fire. He stirred, stirred, and found not a hope of heat or fire.

Maggie said, "Eli come back to bed, I am cold."

Eli said, "Not as cold as we will be if I do not get a fire going in this fireplace."

"Is there no fire at *all* Eli?" asked Maggie. "Not a flicker, the snow is hip deep too," said Eli.

"You stay put and I'll go to Isaac and Mollie's and borrow some fire from them," said Eli. "Hurry back Eli, I'll try to stay warm for you," Maggie said.

Maggie's words warmed Eli even before he put on his buckskin coat. Eli turned to Maggie and said, "I'll be back directly with some fire." He winked at Maggie, and she smiled and winked back.

Eli fought his way through the snow, trying to remember the dips in the land, so he would not be in over his head in a snowdrift. He could make out the fence, in the distance and knew that was the boundary between his land and Isaac and Mollie's land. He trudged along and finally made his way to Isaac's cabin. He knocked on the door and waited for Isaac to answer the door. He dreaded telling his older brother, about letting the fire go out. He knew would get a bit of a chewin', even if it was in gest.

To Eli's relief, Mollie answered instead and said, "Eli, what in the world are you doin' out this mornin'? Come inside and warm, I have some ham, biscuits and gravy, and coffee if you want." Eli thought long and hard about eating but thought about Maggie in the cabin freezing without any fire and said, "I have come to borrow some fire."

Eli inquired about the whereabouts of Isaac, to deflect his embarrassment; Mollie informed him that he had gone to check on his cattle.

"Eli MacGowan, don't tell me you have let your *fire* go out," said Mollie in an astonished tone.

"Yep, I am ashamed to say I have let the fireplace get stone cold, Mollie. Paw or Isaac need not know about this nor any of other my brothers, if you please." Eli said in a pleading tone of voice.

Mollie laughed and said, "Your secret will stay here Eli, it is not a hangin' offense."

"It might as well be to my Paw, you know how he is Mollie," said Eli.

"Yes Eli, I know how the MacGowans are, you remember, I *am* married to Isaac," said Mollie.

"If you please, I'll take my leave and borrow some fire and head back to my cabin before Isaac MacGowan comes and finds me in this predicament," said Eli.

Mollie pointed to a wooden box in the loft and said, "There are corn shucks there, better take plenty, it will take a while to get to your cabin today, on account of the snow." Mollie smiled, she knew the lovebirds had been preoccupied and had not tended to the flame in the fireplace.

Eli wasted no time, grabbed the shucks and stuffed his shirt full, lit one and said, "Thanks Mollie." Off he went.

There is a term used in the valley called "light a shuck" it was meant for times like this, when someone let their fire go cold and had to borrow fire from the neighboring cabin.

Matches were not readily available and Eli knew the importance of keeping the fire going. He blamed himself for neglecting the fire because of honeymooning with Maggie. He thought how this would be his last embarrassing trip to Isaac's place to borrow fire, at least that is what he hoped.

Eli plowed through the snowdrifts, lit one shuck after another, and hoped he would not run out before getting back to his cabin. *Finally*, he was at his cabin door with two shucks to spare, he kicked on the door and Maggie soon flung it open.

Maggie, wrapped in a blanket, had been busy getting the kindling wood ready for starting a fire. Eli wasted no time in grabbing some shucks from his cabin and quickly had a fire going. They waited until a fire was blazing and they put a backlog in the firebox and loaded up the fireplace.

Eli said, "Now we can get some breakfast goin', I am terrible hungry Maggie."

Maggie smiled and dropped the quilt she had draped around her while the fire got going. "Can breakfast keep a while longer," she asked standing naked in front of Eli.

Eli said, "I reckon it will keep a bit Maggie," as he headed for the bed. Maggie turned and jumped in, grabbing the quilt, she covered and watched as Eli shucked off his buckskins. He soon joined her in a similar condition.

Maggie stirred awake with a smile on her sweet face; Eli opened his eyes and felt the warmth of this spring day. He saw Maggie; she was still the same sweet girl that he joined in bed in that cold little cabin in his dreams.

He kissed her and they held each other for a good while. They listened to the river and felt the breeze. Maggie looked at Eli and said, "It sure was cold in that cabin." Eli looked at her with amazement. He smiled at her and said, "Yes, Maggie it *was* cold."

They didn't speak for a bit. Maggie knew Eli was about to use up his patience for the day, lingering here with her, but Eli seemed to have changed some, she thought. Time would tell.

They climbed back into the wagon and headed up the road. They made the settlement by early afternoon and Maggie said, "Things have blossomed around here Eli." He looked around and said, "I guess they have a bit." Maggie said, "A bit; there are five or six buildins' that were not here when I left."

Eli said, "It is getting' to be a regular town here."

Eli laughed and said, "I ain't much for buildins' Maggie. The store is the only buildin' I need here and maybe the church and I guess the school."

Maggie said, "We have a real school? It used to be in the church." Eli replied, "Yes Maggie we have a school and Mister Shanks is still there, last I heard."

Maggie said, "Well, things change I guess Eli."

"Yes they do sweetie, they sure do," said Eli with a smile. The settlement was not the change his thoughts were on today.

"I need to stop in at MacAndrews Store if we have time Eli," said Maggie. He smiled and turned toward the store. Eli's wagon rattled to a halt in front of the MacAndrews Mercantile and General Store. He saw MacAndrews and Corntassel were sitting on the porch chewing and spitting tobacco juice, as usual.

"Well", said MacAndrews "let me roll out the red carpet; it looks like my best customer is back. Welcome Misses MacGowan, good to see you again."

"It is good to be back," she smiled, "Hello there John."

Corntassel smiled and said, "Welcome back; good to see you *both* are back."

Eli and Maggie went into the store he picked up some tobacco and she looked around a bit. "Looks like you have increased your stock a bit MacAndrews."

"It ain't what your boy has in Calhoun but we are doin' our best, "said MacAndrews.

Eli said, "You might want to get some cloth to make new curtains, enough for three winders."

"Three?" said Maggie.

"Yes, I have made two more winders and plan on cuttin' the holes in the cabin this week."

Maggie smiled and said, "Three winders, it will be like daytime in that dark old cabin; that will be nice Eli, really nice." She grabbed him and gave him a peck on the cheek.

MacAndrews saw the affection shown to Eli and raised one bushy red eyebrow in response. Dern you MacAndrews, thought Eli.

Corntassel only grinned, at the two old white men, acting like children.

"Well," said Maggie, "I like this plaid pattern." Maggie handed the cloth to MacAndrews to cut it from the bolt, to the required length.

Maggie picked up a few other things and some peppermint candy for the crowd that would be waiting at the cabin.

Eli paid for the provisions and they headed out of the settlement.

They heard someone shouting *"Maggie, Maggie."* Eli pulled up and they turned to see Becky MacWilliams running to the wagon. She ran up to the wagon and grabbed Maggie by the heel of her shoe. "It's you Maggie, really you. Are you back?"

Maggie looked at Eli, smiled, and said, "I am back for ever Becky."

They laughed and Becky said, "I'll see you tomorrow at dinner. I am ridin' up with the MacGowan women when they take the meal up to the workers."

Maggie pretended not to know about the romancing between her and Jack Mankiller and asked, "Now why are you so much interested in cabin buildin', Becky MacWilliams?"

Becky's face instantly blushed deep red. She smiled and said, "I *know* Eli has told you about me and Jack Mankiller. We are courtin' now." She smiled at Maggie and that told the tale.

Becky said, "I better let you go, I know there is much to do; I'm glad you are back, I have missed you a heap. See you tomorrow." She giggled, and turned to go back home.

Eli thought will we never get home as he slapped the team to life and headed up MacGowan Creek, *finally*.

Maggie said, "Where is Jack buildin' his cabin?"

"Up on Maggie's Branch," Eli said.

"So he will be across the upper corn field?" she asked.

Eli said, "Yep, in the big chestnut stand, a purdy place."

"That was the place you always figured little Gussie would build his cabin, Eli."

He nodded. "Jack picked it, and I told him it was a good place."

"I'm glad Jack will be there," said Maggie.

They turned up the new road up Maggie's Branch and soon came within sight of the cabin builders. The young boys ran down to meet the wagon, and hopped on for a ride. The boys hugged their granny and she planted kisses on all of them. She said, "You boys have grown so much, since the last time I saw you."

Eli was glad to see Maggie happy again and still thought he was *still* a heard headed mule, but was hoping he would forget that, soon.

George, Robert, Timothy, and Thomas MacGowan and Jack Mankiller encircled the wagon. George helped his mother from the wagon and hugged her; she reached for Timothy, then Robert and Thomas.

Then there stood Jack like a statue. Maggie's eyes were full of tears and she went to Jack. She hugged him, kissed him on the cheek, and said, "Thank you Jack Mankiller, once again, you have shown what a friend you are to this family. You are my *brother*."

Jack's eyes welled up and he said. "I am glad to see you and Eli have been made whole again."

Maggie hugged Jack again and cleared her throat, wiped her eyes and said, "Let's see this cabin of yours *Jack Mankiller*."

She stood between Jack and Eli and took a hand from each and they strolled with easy strides, up to peruse the cabin.

It was a *great day*!

CHAPTER TWENTY
BROKEN LIMBS

Maggie, Jack, and Eli walked around and checked the cabin that would soon be Jack's home. Maggie was pleased with the work. She could see Eli's hand in every detail. He may have only supervised the work, for the most part, but she could see his good work through his sons and grandsons.

She said, "This cabin is laid out well, the light will wake you in the morning and the breeze will cool it in the summer. You all have done well." Maggie said, "I had always hoped one of my sons would build on this site but I reckon that my brother, Jack Mankiller will be even better."

Jack *was* like a brother to Eli and Maggie. They had been through some good times and some very hard times together in the early days at Watauga Valley.

Eli said, "We will need to get the planting done as soon as the cabin is finished unless we plan on goin' hungry this winter." They all chuckled and headed to Eli and Maggie's cabin.

Maggie said, "I need to get supper started men." Eli and Jack looked at each other and grinned, they knew their cooking days were over and that their stomachs would be grateful.

As they rode up to the cabin, Maggie asked, "Where's Dawg?" Eli and Jack looked at each other with questioning expressions, what to say they wondered in silence.

Maggie said again, "Where is Dawg?"

Eli said, "Maggie there is no easy way to say this, I know that old dog meant a lot to you and Gussie; but Dawg is gone. A rattler bit him a while back and we buried him over by the big chestnut, by the branch."

The tears welled up and overflowed down Maggie's cheeks. She said, "I loved that old dog; he was Gussie's best friend in this world."

"Now he *is* Gussie's best friend in the heaven," said Eli. They embraced and held each other all the way to the cabin.

Jack trying to change the mood, said, "Let me get a fire started in the stove."

Maggie, in agreement said, "Enough of this; he was an old dog and had a good life." Eli agreed, "He was a good companion most of the time, when no one else was around."

They all smiled. Maggie and Jack knew what he was trying to say was that he missed the old dog something fierce but would not admit the fact. It was just Eli's way.

Maggie cooked a meal that Eli thought was the best he had ever had. Jack also gorged on Maggie's cooking, sat back, and enjoyed one of Rachel's fried pies and a hot cup of Maggie's coffee.

Eli said, "Maggie come sit with us and let's talk for a while." She paused because it was against her nature to relax before washing the supper plates, but she said, "I might as well, the dishes can wait a while."

She lit a broom straw from the lamp and lit Eli and Jacks pipes. She pulled up an Eli MacGowan handmade chair, and sat for some conversation. Eli smiled and said, "Maggie I have so much missed this time we shared every evenin'."

She smiled and said, "I missed it too."

They hugged up and kissed, nearly cooing like mourning doves, at each other.

Jack said, "Am I gonna have to *leave?*"

Maggie and Eli laughed and in unison said "*no!*"

Maggie said, "Do you remember when we were young and Becky Walker and I would follow you two around and giggle. I still don't see what we saw in either of you," she said in jest.

"Why I was a fine cut of a man," said Eli. Now Jack was pretty middlin' in looks but he made up for his lack of looks with his good huntin' skills."

"Middlin'," said Jack, "I seem to remember fightin' off the girls, in the valley, all the time."

"All right," said Maggie, "you were both fine lookin' boys; you would have to have been to have fine ladies like Becky and me."

They all laughed, and shortly Jack's smile faded to a stoic look. "He said you know I still miss Becky Walker, wonder what life we would have had, if things had worked out different."

"Becky was a sweet girl," said Eli, "I just don't know why things like that happen Jack," said Maggie.

Eli looked with sadness and said, "If we ever figure that out, we will be some smart people for sure."

"Well," said Maggie, "changin' the subject, what is this about Becky MacWilliams, Jack?" Jack actually blushed a bit; Eli enjoyed watching him, squirming in his chair, as he thought about how to respond.

"Yep, Maggie, I aim to marry her if she will have me. I feel for her like no woman since Becky Walker. I have searched the valley and found the woman I have been lookin' for, *right here*."

Eli thought how Jack worded that good enough. He must have it bad for Becky to be this mushy.

Maggie smiled her sweet smile at Jack and said, "I am so happy for you Jack, and for Becky. She will have you I am sure. You are a fine man Jack, and she is a fine woman. It will be good to have you for neighbors. Becky will be good to talk to and Eli will have his brother close by too."

Eli thought this is enough of this talk for tonight and stood up, rapped the tobacco from his pipe into the stove. He said, "It has been a long day, time for me to get to sleep.

Jack said, "I guess you will want the feather bed back?"

"Yep, if you can stand sleepin' on the corn shuck bed tonight, tomorrow we will bring in the feather bed that Isaac and Rachel sent with us," said Eli.

Eli and Jack went to bed and shortly, both snoring while Maggie finished cleaning up the supper plates. She thought it was sweet music to her ears, as she soon followed them in slumber.

After a peaceful sleep, the morning came and Eli woke by the sound of Maggie cooking breakfast or was he dreaming. No, it was Maggie back where she belonged, he thought, with a smile.

He could hear the sweet sound of her humming a tune while she rattled the coffee pot. The aroma was all Eli needed to roll out of the feather bed and slip on his clothes.

He walked over to Maggie, pecked her on the cheek, gave her a hug, and said, "It's good to have you home, and I'll never get tired of sayin' that Maggie."

Maggie grinned and said, "It is good to be home Eli, I have missed this old cabin more than you can imagine, so many memories here." Eli said, "Memories, some good, some bad." Maggie said, "They are all our memories, Eli, good and bad, they are ours."

Jack said, "If you two lovebirds want me to leave, I could Maggie"

Maggie said, "Jack, you and Eli are going to have to settle down; there is a lady on the place now. You two need to get over here and eat, the boys will be here and ready to get to work on the cabin shortly. I am startin' to think you boys have turned triflin' on me."

Eli and Jack laughed and took turns washing up for breakfast. They wolfed down the breakfast and talked between gulps. It was the most pleasant breakfast Eli could remember in a long while. It was good it was very good.

Jack said," The wagons are headed up the holler."

"Well, let's get to work," said Eli. Maggie chimed in saying "where do I start?" Eli said, "The old Guernsey would probably be glad to have your soft hands back under her again." Maggie said," I'll be glad to see my old friend again, there is much to do in this cabin too but I'll treasure every bit that I do. You two get to work; go on, get out of here." She pretended to swat them on the rear with the broom and cackled loudly.

Eli and Jack headed to the cabin site, joined the boys there, and went immediately to work.

Maggie smiled as she briskly strode towards the barn to milk, she pulled up the stool and she was sure she saw the old Guernsey smile at her.

"I'm back old gal have you missed me?"

A loud "moo" was her answer; Maggie took that as a yes. She finished her milking and fed the animals in the barn, they all were glad to see her. She patted some on the head and talked in her soothing sweet voice to the others.

Things were back to normal around the MacGowan Place again. At least as normal as they ever would be. Maggie strolled up the cabin and strained the milk, poured it into a clay jug and took it to the springhouse. As she went back to the cabin, she took inventory of what she needed to do the rest of the day.

"Let's see, churn, clean up the cabin, and wash the bed clothes that should be enough for today," she said to herself.

She worked away the early morning, sat on the porch, and started churning. She always enjoyed this chore, it produced sweet butter and buttermilk, nothing like fresh buttermilk, she thought. She had done this hundreds of times but today was special, she sat on her porch on a beautiful spring day and listened to Eli, Jack, her sons, and grandsons working on Jack Mankiller's cabin.

She found a rhythm and hummed a tune. She could hear the axes chopping and chipping the logs at the cabin site and drifted off in thought.

She was back at Watauga sitting with her father and mother waiting on Eli MacGowan. She could remember the wait, it seemed endless, and then the knock came on the door.

William Johnson walked over and opened the door. Eli stood in the door, tall and confident. That was Eli, she thought, always confident. Maggie's father stood and sternly looked at Eli, making him somewhat uncomfortable.

"Well, Eli what can I do for you?"

"Eli said I need to talk to you sir."

"Well, let's take a walk and we can talk," said William Johnson as they walked out, strolled over to the bench under the big white oak, and took a seat.

Eli was trying his best to be manly and William Johnson was trying his best to enjoy the situation, without showing it to Eli.

"How is the pipe playin' comin' Eli?" asked William.

"Oh, purty good I reckon," said Eli.

William said, "We could use some rain you think, Eli?"

"I reckon we could, Mister Johnson."

"Well, what you got on your mind, Eli?"

There was a long pause, and Eli cleared his throat and said, "I guess I'll just say what I have to say." Another long pause, "That would be good Eli," said William.

"Mister Johnson, the day you first pulled your wagon onto our place, I saw Maggie, and fell in love with her. I didn't know it was love right then, but I figured it out, shortly," said Eli.

Eli continued, "I can promise you some things right here; I promise to always treat her with kindness, to love her, to provide a good livin' for her and to protect her with my life."

"I'll try my best to never do anything that will bring shame to your house, or to your good name. I reckon that is about all I can say. Can I marry Maggie?"

William paused, and Eli with that pause, Eli felt beads of sweat popping out on his forehead. He spoke, "Eli, I have always wanted the best for my children as any father would. We have watched you and Maggie for near on two years now, her Momma always hoped you two would get hitched. Heck, Eli I reckon I hoped the same."

"All I ask is that you treat her good, and try to follow what the "Good Book" teaches, in your life, and love The Lord. That is about all I have to say lad."

William said, "You better get down there and fetch Maggie before she explodes."

He extended his hand and Eli shook it firmly. William said, "Welcome to the family Eli; I'll always treat you like a son. Now get goin'."

Maggie was peeking out the window and could see Eli taking his long lanky strides as he confidently walked toward her. She thought she could have counted all his teeth, due to the big smile on his face. He knocked on the door and her mother opened the door and said, "I guess he said yes?"

"Yes'um he did, I reckon you will have me in the family," he said with a smile, and she grabbed him, hugged him, and said. "If I could have picked a man for Maggie, it would be you Eli. You are a fine young man. I am proud to have you marry my daughter. Welcome to our family Eli."

He was looking at Maggie and he could see she was smiling with pride. He walked over and hugged her and said," I reckon we will have to get a preacher, if we aim to get hitched."

"Hang on there Mister MacGowan there are some things we need to get arranged," said Maggie's mother. "Like a weddin' young man."

Eli knew he had lots to do before he would marry Maggie; he had land to clear, a cabin to build, and crops to get in the ground. That would take most of the spring, so they planned to get married in the summer.

Maggie remembered how hard Eli worked. He was determined to do most of the work himself. That is what he did, his brothers, father and her father helped with the cabin building. Eli did the rest.

He had a fine crop in the field and a garden that would keep Maggie busy. He had a barn almost built and had acquired a cow and two hogs.

The time came when Eli told Maggie that they had reached the place where the wedding planning could begin. The preacher announced the wedding date at services a week before.

There were many traditions that Eli and Maggie's parents had endured to wed. Some traditions went away, others blended with the American traditions in the new world. One that survived was the tradition of foot washing. The night before the wedding, Maggie and her female family members and friends gathered at the Johnson cabin for the prenuptial festivities. The foot washing began as Maggie placed her feet into a tub of water. Into that tub, they placed her mother's ring. The young unmarried women would wash her feet by searching for the ring in the water. The lucky girl who found the ring would be the next to marry, or so said tradition.

While Maggie was being entertained, Eli was enduring his own traditions at his brother Isaac's cabin. The married men subjected Eli to many jokes. They also shared the traditional meal and several wee drams of William MacGowan whisky.

The day of the wedding was exciting for Eli, Maggie, and the rest of the Watauga settlement. Her female friends and family escorted Maggie to the church. She walked as they threw flower petals in her path. The men folk all secured the pigs of the community to ensure none would cross her path, which would be bad luck.

The Watauga Church was small in stature but large in character. Mostly the skilled hands of the MacGowans had built it. Eli had left his mark on the joinery of the logs as well as the pews. Single logs of chestnut carefully carved served as benches and were a solid place to park ones rear for Sunday services. The interior was dim due to having only four windows; coal oil lamps subsidized the lighting. In the early days, pine torches lit the saintly structure and had left their blackened stains on the walls.

Today the church had the scent of honeysuckle and had decorations of laurel and rhododendron blooms. The benches sat full of smiling Scots, dressed in their Sunday garments.

Maggie was dressed in her mother's wedding dress; it was a plain white dress with a blue ribbon around her waist. The lace veil didn't conceal her smile and it only widened when she saw Eli standing up front with the preacher.

Eli stood proudly in his kilt that his father had worn when he wed his mother. The finely woven wool tartan, used only for the most important occasions, because it was one of the few remnants left from the journey from Scotland. Angus MacGowan had carried this garment, on the long journey, from Dalwhinnie to America.

Eli beamed at Maggie, as they each solemnly spoke their vows. Once the vows were complete, Angus played the pipes. All who attended thought it was the grandest wedding they had ever seen.

Eli was just relieved to have survived the ceremony. Maggie was now Eli's wife and she felt her life was perfect at that moment.

The crowd feasted after the ceremony, it lasted into the night and the last deed to do was the traditional serenading of the new couple. Tradition was to ride the bride and groom around in a chair, raised high by the raucous crowd, the path lit by the pine torches they carried. They danced the couple around while they tried not to fall off the chairs. They sang songs and tried their best to embarrass the naïve couple.

Maggie remembered how they danced them both to the door of their new cabin and sat them down. Eli picked her up and carried her across the threshold, because if the bride tripped, that would be bad luck. Eli stepped inside with Maggie and closed the door.

Maggie remembered how innocent they both were and she remembered that night and how frightened she was, Eli was jittery too, she recalled.

Eli lit the candles and they sat and looked at each other for a good while, not really knowing what to do next, since they had never been alone together in a room.

She had only kissed Eli on the mouth three times, not counting the wedding. They grinned at each other and Eli said I guess we need to get in bed. Which they did; they figured the rest out as the night went on into the day.

Maggie smiled and thought how she had slept with Eli for over fifty years. Taking out the last few years due to his stubbornness, and the times he was gone off to war, she still felt her best when she was next to him.

"Maggie, *Maggie MacGowan*" she heard someone shout at her. She snapped from her daydream and saw Becky MacWilliams coming up to the front of the cabin. She had a big smile and it caused Maggie to respond likewise.

"Well, hello Becky, come on up and sit for a while." said Maggie. Becky stepped up onto the porch and sat beside Maggie. They enjoyed each other's company for a good while, catching up on the years of lost time. Maggie said, "I was just thinkin' about when me and Eli got married. I hear there might be another weddin' soon," Maggie said with a giggle.

"Wonder who?" said Becky. "Oh I think you know," said Maggie," if Jack Mankiller ever asks a certain good woman to be his wife."

They giggled like schoolgirls. He said, "If you would have him he reckoned he would marry you," said Maggie. "I reckon I'll have him *if* he ever asks me," said Becky.

"Jack is like Eli, you can't rush him, he studies things out and once he has made up his mind that is it."

They giggled some more.

"Well, Maggie we're gettin' ready to eat dinner at Jack's cabin, Eli sent me to fetch you over."

Maggie said "let's go then Becky; maybe Mankiller will be in the askin' mood today." They giggled and left for the cabin.

By the time Maggie and Becky arrived, the rest of the Clan MacGowan had washed up and were sitting down at the table for dinner. Eli sat at the head as was tradition and Maggie sat to his right after serving the men.

Eli looked down the table and thought what a fine crop of youngins' Maggie and me have made. He felt a little sad missing his sons and daughters that were away or the ones that were in heaven, he took a deep breath and smiled. He knew it was sinful to be proud, but he hoped The Almighty would forgive him for this feeling today.

Maggie swarmed around the table like a queen bee with the younger women listening to her every word. They all loved Maggie and were glad she was back to help dispense some wisdom when needed.

Jack just sat and admired Becky; Eli nudged him and asked, "When are you goin' to ask her Jack?" Jack replied, "I'm still stalkin' her Eli but I'm closin' in on her. I want to be sure before askin'; this is a considerable lot of thinkin' for me to do."

"I think you're just a wee bit a feared there Jack Mankiller. I have seen you fight to the death and look less affright than you look right now, "said Eli.

"You know me pretty good Eli, it is a frightful thing to do, ain't felt like this about a woman in a long time, she's the woman but I just don't want to rush things. I'll pull the trigger when I'm sure."

"Don't rush it Jack, but waitin' ain't makin' you any younger, old boy. You might wait so long as to not have any bullets left in that gun."

"She *is* awful young Eli," said Jack.

"She is waitin' you better not fool around and let some other feller take her from you, better be thinkin' about askin' purty soon," said Eli.

Maggie handed the bread to Jack and Eli. She smiled, and said, "You two sure look serious, and *doesn't* that Becky look pretty today?"

The two old coots only grinned at Maggie and Jack said, "them biscuits look mighty good there Maggie."

She knew what they were discussing and she hoped that Eli was workin' on Jack to nudge him along. Of course, knowing Jack, he might need a pick handle across his hard head to get him to move along.

"Time to ask the blessin'," said Eli; they all joined hands and gave thanks for the meal.

The boys ate their fills and started back to work on the cabin. Eli watched as one by one the young MacGowans joined in the work. The progress was good, and Eli expected they would be finished in another day or two. He stood up from the table and admired the work.

"That, my friend is good, very good", Eli said.

That night Jack went to court Becky *and* eat supper with her and the rest of the Corntassel bunch.

Eli and Becky had the place to themselves. After supper, they sat on the porch, Eli smoking his pipe and Maggie just enjoying the company and the view.

"Eli you know that when I went to live with Isaac and Rachel I was so alone and heartbroken. I felt like I had to go or stay here to watch you slowly wither away. I could not bear to see you that way anymore, so I left."

Maggie continued, "I stopped at the graves and said goodbye. I had slung some clothes in a blanket and walked down the road to the settlement with Dawg by my side."

"I asked John Corntassel to take me to Timothy's cabin and sent Dawg back to you 'cause I figured you would need a friend," said Maggie.

"I was cryin' night and day and didn't want to upset the youngins', so I asked Timothy to take me to Isaacs. You know how Isaac is, he was not much help but Rachel became a good friend, as well, just like a daughter. She was there to talk with and listen to me; she was a shoulder to cry upon," said Maggie.

"I started to feel better after a month or so, but never quit missin' you Eli, nor did I ever give up on you. I prayed for you mornin' and night. I had faith that you would find your way to me and years later, there you were riding in that wagon down Main Street coming to take me home."

Maggie took Eli's rough old hand, squeezed it, and said, "I'll not leave you again Eli MacGowan." Eli grinned and squeezed gently in return.

Eli said, "Maggie I was a stranger to myself after the youngins' died. I couldn't get my head cleared; it was like I was walkin' around in the dark."

"Most days I just worked and tried not to think any more than I had to, but just mostly worked."

"I remember the day I came home and saw the note you left on the table. I still have it in my Bible. I know it word for word," Eli said.

"It said I know you are still a good man Eli, but you have been given more than you can carry now. When your load becomes lighter, and the path becomes brighter, I pray you will find your way back to me. Love, Maggie."

"I read it a dozen times the first days you were gone, I couldn't understand what it meant, but it came to me one day on the mountain and I knowed I had to wake up and go get you."

"In the beginning, people from the church would come and visit me, I would not talk much and they would leave. My sons would come and talk, I had nothing to say nor did I want to hear anything they had to say. Then no one came. I was here with Dawg."

Eli said, "Dawg listened to me on my terms, he didn't offer help, and he was there to let me think things through in my own way. I'm afraid that I wasn't always good to the old boy, but I guess he knew that I was not myself and overlooked lots of things I did and said."

"I remember one dreary winter afternoon; I walked up to the Indian bluffs and sat. I didn't bother to build a warmin' fire. I just sat cold, dark, bitter, and miserable.

I started to cry, I cried way into the night."

"I figured it was time me and The Almighty came to blows. It was goin' to be better, or I was leavin' this misery for good."

Eli continued, "Then I got up threw a rope over a stout lookin' chestnut limb and tied it off, put it around my neck. Lookin' over the valley, I wondered what my youngins' and their families were doin'. I wondered what you were doin'. I prayed that you all would forgive me. That was the first time I had prayed in years."

"Then I jumped! Off the short ledge I went, thinking this would end my pain."

"Now Maggie, I have never known a chestnut limb to be weak but this one that I picked snapped when the rope drew tight around my neck, and I fell to the ledge below."

"The fall knocked me out cold. I lay there all night and woke up the next morning with Dawg lyin' on top of me. I reckon he kept me from freezin' to death. I rolled him off me and sat up."

"Dawg just sat there lookin' at me like I was a fool. He was right, I *was* a fool!"

Eli said, "Anyone who thinks they can play God and decide when they are leavin' this world *is* a fool. It was not my time, I figured. So I just sat there for a while and thought."

"The sun broke over the ridge and little shafts of light shot down the valley. It was the most glorious morning of my life. It was really the first day of my new life. In the brightness, in my mind I could see your note; this was the first step to me findin' my way, Maggie."

"Then I felt a pain in my arm and looked down to see I had broken my arm, so I tied my wrist off with a rope to a saplin' and pulled it back in place the best I could and made a brace out of the chestnut limb and the rope I had tried to use for my hangin'."

I said, "well Dawg, if I ain't broke nothin' else, I reckon we better get some breakfast and see what this day will have for us. That was the same day Jack Mankiller showed up."

"Was it a chance happenin' that Jack showed that very day, had had I been sent a guide to help me find the rest of my way back to you?"

Maggie cried and fell at Eli's feet; she placed her head on Eli's knees. She said, "how could I live without you Eli, how could I live without you in my life."

Eli placed his big hands under her chin, gently cradled her soft face, and said, "I'll not leave you again Maggie MacGowan, not until The Almighty comes and takes me home."

She rose and sat in his lap and they embraced without talking for a long time. Maggie said, "We better get some sleep Eli and goosed him in the ribs. He jumped and said we will not have to go directly to sleep, will we?"

She smiled and said, "No I guess not, since we *are* alone tonight." They got up from the porch and closed the door giggling and hoped Jack would not be in a hurry to come back tonight.

CHAPTER TWENTYONE
JACK AND BECKY

The summer rolled into early fall; the leaves hinted at their glory to come and the mornings were becoming crisp and cool. The cabin was finished as well as a barn and smokehouse. Jack and Eli had built all the furnishings, to fill the cabin. Jack was proud of his new home, his first place of his own. Eli and Maggie were proud for Jack. Maggie just wondered if Jack Mankiller would *ever* have a wife, namely Becky MacWilliams, to finish filling the new cabin.

It was a glorious Sunday morning in the Hiwassee Valley and everyone was dressed in their finest clothes. Jack had become a regular at church, and sat next to Becky, Eli, and Maggie. Things were becoming routine; and then it happened.

Jack Mankiller rose, after the closing of the services, and the entire congregation became quiet. Jack cleared his throat and spoke; "I want to speak from my heart to you all."

"I came to this valley as a stranger to all except for Eli and Maggie MacGowan. All I met welcomed me. Eli MacGowan gave me a place to build a cabin, and the MacGowans built it for me. I have been helped beyond any man's dreams. If I die today, I'll die a happy man."

There are some other words I need to say, to Becky MacWilliams. Becky, I have wanted you as my wife from the first day I saw you. Today, I ask you to be my woman, if you will have me."

He waited for Becky to respond.

Becky started to weep, and Jack looked bewildered; would she not have him, he wondered?

Becky spoke, "Jack Mankiller I love you and would be honored to be your wife, I had just about thought, you would never ask." They hugged and the church laughed, cheered and swarmed the betrothed couple.

Eli hugged Jack and said, "It took you long enough Mankiller, I guess you just needed extra time to study this out." Jack just smiled and said, "I owe this all to you, Eli."

That was all that needed to be said, between those two.

Becky and Maggie made plans for the wedding, one that would be an unrivaled event, in this valley.

Eli and Jack cleared out the barn for the after wedding dance. They moved all the animals to Jack's barn; they covered the whisky still with blankets so its presence would not offend anyone, mainly Pastor Emmons. They had to do a considerable amount shoveling. This was to ensure no foot would have a manure encounter, while dancing.

Maggie and Becky completed the decorating in the barn, as well as the church. It was an impressive sight.

Eli and Maggie, thought it would be a fun time for all, he had the boys coming for entertainment and he planned to break out some of the Scotch whisky he had set aside, for the last 5 years, aging to perfection, for an occasion like this.

The day of the wedding came, and Jack and Eli were jumpy as cornered rats. Jack said, "I ain't ever been married Eli, how is a man to act?"

"Well, Jack just take care of her, and you got to sweet talk her some too."

Jack looked puzzled and asked, "When do I do *that* Eli?"

"You'll know Jack, you'll find her cryin' for no good reason, just figure you have either said somethin' wrong, or not said somethin' right. It takes lots of practice, to figure out the difference, I ain't exactly figured it all out yet," said Eli.

"Dern! Eli, how am I gonna figure it out; I'm gettin' to be an old man." said Jack.

Eli said, "She'll get you trained up in a few years, or so. Just look sad, and say you're sorry, when you ain't sure what to do."

Jack rubbed his whiskers and said," its dern hard to figure, ain't it Eli."

"It sure is my friend; just go huntin' a lot; the more you're gone the less likely you are to mess up."

They broke into belly laughs. This drew a frustrated look from Maggie, who was putting the finishing touches on the church decorations. Eli took the look, from Maggie, as a come help, or get in trouble look.

"Jack did you see that look from Maggie?"

"Yes," said Jack.

"I know what it means; it took me years to learn it, but I know I better get down there and help."

"I'll come too Eli," said Jack, with a smile.

The wedding day arrived for Jack Mankiller and Becky MacWilliams. The ceremony was a solemn and sweet rite; there were smiles *and* tears in the congregation. Becky was a vision; she was as pretty as anyone could remember seeing her. Even Jack had cleaned up and dressed up, and looked about as good as he could, Eli thought.

Then the celebration moved to the MacGowan barn. It was a lively place for sure that afternoon. For this special day, it was acceptable for the men to have a wee dram of Scotch whisky to celebrate. Some had more than a wee dram, especially Pastor Emmons.

Eli thought how Pastor Emmons was not as well acquainted with the spirits of the jug, as he was with the spirits of the Bible. He became a little loud, and drew one or two of "those looks" from his wife, who didn't seem entertained, by his behavior.

Jack and Eli sipped only a wee bit, as too much would spoil their dancing skills and they did intend to dance. Eli grabbed Maggie and spun her around the barn, they wheeled and laughed and danced, as much as their sore joints would allow. Jack and Becky tried to keep up, and did an admirable job.

Eli and the boys played tune after tune until they had played their entire repertoire and some tunes twice.

It was the most fun Eli could remember having in years. The crowd thinned some, and they allowed Jack and Becky to have the barn floor, to close the evening.

They did a reel; they grinned and held each other close. They bowed to the guests, as they finished.

The chairs came and they hoisted up the newlyweds and they carried both to the cabin door, thankfully, mainly by the most sober attendees. They were gently set down on the cabin porch. They held hands and turned to crowd and bowed, he picked Becky up and carried her into the cabin, and closed the door.

Maggie and Eli led their animals formerly housed in Jack's barn, to make room for the hoedown, back to their barn and they talked.

"It was a good day Eli," said Maggie. "A very good day," said Eli.

They walked to their cabin and turned to look at Jack and Becky's cabin. They could see a glimmer of light from the window. Maggie said, "Now we have neighbors Eli." "Friends and neighbors," said Eli.

"Jack Mankiller is a married man," said Maggie. "I would have never believed it." "Me either" said Eli, "me either."

The next day, Eli and Maggie went to MacAndrews Store, to get some supplies. They bumped down the road towards the store; Eli wondered if Jack would be up to honeymooning, at his age.

Maggie giggled and said, "Age ain't slowed you down none MacGowan. Well, maybe some, but not much."

Eli puffed up his chest and said, "You have married a *man* for sure Maggie." She elbowed him in the ribs, shook her head, and giggled. They continued to bump their way to MacAndrews Store.

They pulled up to the store, tied off the horses and saw John Corntassel sitting on the porch. "Mornin' John" said Maggie.

"Mornin'" said Corntassel. Eli nodded to the Indian.

Eli noticed John was holding something under his coat. "What

172

do you have there Corntassel?" asked Eli.

"Oh, just somethin' that old dog of yours left behind." He held out his hand and there was a tiny version of Dawg.

Eli grinned and Maggie grabbed the fuzzy pup and snuggled him to her face. The pup whimpered his approval, of Maggie's affection.

John said, "He is that old dog's pup, no doubt Eli."

Eli and Maggie both agreed. "He is exactly like Dawg," said Maggie.

"He's yours Eli, if you want him," said Corntassel.

"We *do* need a dog Eli, said Maggie."

Without even a thought Eli said, "We'll take him."

Maggie looked *astonished*, at the lack of negotiation needed, to reach the decision about the pup. She was *so astonished*, that his words didn't take root for a bit. Maggie repeated, "He sure looks like Dawg don't he Eli? Did you just say we can take him home, Eli?"

Eli smiled and said, "Yep, I reckon he's Dawg's for sure. Let Corntassel have him back, while we get our supplies."

Maggie reluctantly handed him back to John Corntassel and told the pup, she would be back shortly.

They packed the wagon with the supplies, picked up the pup, and headed home. The little pup was unnamed; Eli figured Maggie would want to name him. Dawg was fine with him.

Sure enough Maggie said, "We need to name this one Eli and it ain't gonna be called Dawg. Why don't you pick a name Eli?"

"I ain't much on namin' animals, you know Maggie; you better pick one, "said Eli.

"This old road sure is rocky, Eli," said Maggie.

"Better than muddy up to the axles, I reckon," said Eli.

Maggie squealed, with excitement and said, "How 'bout Rocky; then Eli; let's call him Rocky."

"Fine with me," said Eli, "Rocky it is then."

"Howdy little Rocky," said Maggie as she stroked the little fuzzy pup.

They neared Jack and Becky's cabin; they glanced and saw that it showed no signs of life yet. Jack and Maggie looked at each other and grinned.

They pulled up to the cabin. Maggie placed the pup on the porch, took some boards and boxed him in so he would stay put. She put a bowl of water down and fed him a piece of cornbread for his supper.

"There little Rocky, eat your supper," said Maggie. He was a happy little pup, thought Eli, a lucky one too, to have Maggie taking care of him.

Eli and Maggie sat down to supper and talked about the events of the past days. Maggie said, "Eli, we need to start havin' a hoedown every month or two, like we used to, it would be good."

Eli agreed and said, "We will let things settle down with Jack and Becky; maybe in the spring, that would be good Maggie."

CHAPTER TWENTYTWO
PROTÉGÉS ARE DELIVERED

The days rolled into months and spring came around. There was lots of excitement on MacGowan Creek, on this fine late winter morning, as Jack and Becky were visiting for breakfast. They had just finished eating and Becky grinned and said, "I have to tell you both, that me and Jack are goin' to have a youngin'."

Jack sat there grinning like a possum as Maggie and Eli stood and hugged the couple. Eli said, "You old coot, gonna be a daddy, that is good word indeed."

"I expect it will be here in late summer," said Becky.

"Jack Mankiller a father," said Maggie, "I am so happy for you two." She hugged Becky again. "We will need to get started makin' some baby clothes and blankets."

Eli still in disbelief of the situation, stood grinning at Jack said, "Jack and me will need to build a crib, I reckon."

"I have news too said Eli. You know that Tom White, the postmaster, sent word yesterday, that my two sons in Georgia are comin' back here, to settle and raise their families. They will be here in March they said."

Tom White, who was the husband of Eli and Maggie's daughter Gillian, was very happy to deliver the news.

Gillian was so happy to know her two younger brothers Lemuel and Newton would be returning with their wives and young families.

Eli said, "They have done well in Dahlonega, and had made enough money to come back, and start a business."

"Well then, we will need to get cabins built for them Eli," said Jack.

"Where *will* they build?" Eli questioned, aloud.

"I reckon I'll let them have land down the creek; there is plenty of good bottom land when it is cleared."

Eli and Maggie could barely conceal their happiness.

The news of their sons returning, *and* of Jack and Becky expecting, made for a good day indeed, thought Eli.

Eli proudly stood up and said, "There is much to do, we need to get started. Jack will you walk with me, and help me study out some cabin sites for them?" Jack nodded his agreement to the mission and they walked down MacGowan Creek and looked at the land.

Eli knew they would want a site where they could build all the necessary structures, and have a good spring nearby. Sites that would be sheltered from the north winds, and open to the south sun in winter. Eli figured he would give each about a hundred acres, that should be enough to make a livin', he thought.

The day came and Eli and Maggie looked down the valley and saw two wagons, loaded to near overflowing, with children and belongings, coming up the rocky road. It *was* Lemuel and Newton coming home.

Eli and Maggie walked as briskly as their old legs would carry them down to meet the wagons. They had never met the boy's wives or seen any of the children. It would be a happy time for all.

The wagons rattled to a stop, side by side. Eli and Maggie stood in front of the horses, just admiring the sight before them. Another piece of the MacGowan Clan is reunited, they thought. What a sight to see, for Eli and Maggie. They just stood and admired the moment; frozen in time, they were, afraid to blink for fear of finding it only a dream; but it was *not* a dream. They were *truly* here.

Lemuel or "Lem" as all knew him was a tall stocky built man with a broad ruddy face and auburn hair.

Newton or "Newt" was a little shorter with brown hair and a red beard.

Lem and Newt hopped down from the wagon, turned and helped their wives down. Maggie was glad to see that living in a heathen place, had not caused her sons to lose their manners.

They took their wives by the hand and strolled over to Eli and Maggie. Maggie hugged each, as Eli stood there watching. They walked to their father and shook his hand. Eli said with joy in his voice, "Good to have you boys back, we have lots to talk about, I reckon."

Maggie said, "Eli give them a hug." Eli grinned, as did the sons. He grabbed each by the neck and hugged them close; for fear of letting them get away again, to Georgia.

Eli cried. The boys had never seen their father like this, showing emotion *and* affection. It was awkward at first to the two, but they responded in kind, sobbing with their father for a good while.

The sight put Maggie over the edge as she started crying, as she hugged her two new daughters, the wives of her sons she had never met.

After introductions of the wives, Eli looked into the wagon and saw more MacGowans. Newt said, "I have five sons and two daughters."

Lem said, "I have four sons and three daughters."

One by one, they made introductions of the grandchildren. After the introductions and generous hugs and kisses, Maggie thought, how fine is this next generation of MacGowans, and now they are here to join her grand children down the creek.

Eli and Maggie heard each name and both thought, how in the world, would they remember them all. It would come with time they thought.

Eli did a count and found it short by the numbers given. One boy each was missin', he thought. He inquired and learned they were bringing the other wagon, but had lingered with their cousins a bit longer, at their farms.

Eli heard the sound of a wagon coming up the road, looked, and saw his last two grandsons, coming his way.

The wagon pulled up and the first boy came up, as the other was tying off the horses. He was Newt's oldest son, they hugged and chatted and he joined his family.

The last boy finally made an appearance. Maggie almost fainted as she grabbed Eli by the arm to steady herself. She looked at this lanky fourteen-year-old boy coming to her; she saw Eli MacGowan made over.

His confidence was beyond his years; he strolled over to Maggie and said I'm William Elijah MacGowan. Maggie was speechless, as well as breathless. He even *sounded* like Eli as he spoke, his eyes, his hair, his mannerisms, were identical to Eli MacGowans.

Eli said, "ain't you gonna hug William too, Maggie?"

Maggie woke from her stupor, grabbed him, and hugged him.

He softly said, "Good to meet you, Granny MacGowan."

Maggie said, "Good to meet you too, William."

"They call me Billy," he said.

"Well, Billy it will be," said Maggie.

Eli hugged Billy and told him, like all the others, how proud he was to meet him.

Maggie said, "What fine youngins'. Oh, I have so much spoilin' to get caught up on with this bunch. So much to catch up on," she said.

Eli agreed there would be lots to teach the youngins' about life: he was beaming with pride, as was Maggie. They chatted a while and Eli, as was his usual matter of fact way, said, "There is much to do. We better get started."

Newt and Lem agreed, and they walked with Eli to see the cabin sites.

Eli noticed young Billy was in tow, and he motioned for him to join the group. They walked and talked about the happenings in Georgia. Eli, without going into too much detail, tried to catch them up on the news around home.

Back at the cabin, Maggie was a queen bee again, talking and cooking, learning names, learning more of her new family members. She was happy, and knew Eli well enough to know he was happy too.

Eli, Lem, Newt, and Billy sat a huge chestnut stump, on the side of the ridge, looking at the land. The boys told of their good fortune in Georgia. How they had landed good claims, worked hard and had done well. They had made money not just from gold, but also from providing for the needs of the people there.

They brought in sawmill equipment, established a good business and sold the business along with their claims and homes and decided to come home to start a business here.

Eli was impressed to listen to his sons who had left as boys and had become men. Billy was quietly listening to the exchange of words.

"Paw," said Newt, "what we have done is buy new steam equipment, and we plan to start a sawmill business, to cut wood for homes, that the settlers comin' in will need."

"We have the equipment comin' on barges from Knoxville. It should be here by the end of the month." Newt continued.

"We plan to build the mill in the settlement by the Federal Road, not far from the river. We expect a railroad will be comin' through the valley soon, and they will need crossties, for the rails."

"We expect to cut 'em," said Lem. "We have figured this every way we could think, Paw. We can make a livin', we know."

Eli studied the words he had filtered through his head and said, "I reckon you boys know more about the lumber business than me. I say you will both make a go of it."

They told Eli that they would like to live with their brothers families, and if they didn't mind, with him, until the equipment came. They said the first boards sawed would be for their homes.

"We will not build a cabin Paw; we will build the first board houses in this settlement." Eli grinned and rubbed his whiskers, "I'll want to learn this way of buildin'," he said.

"We learned it some in Georgia; we think we can figure the rest out, as we go. Billy can figure a house pattern for us and we will cut it and build it."

Eli said, "Billy can do that?"

"William is a real smart boy Paw, even if he ain't mine," said Newt. "Lem has sired a prize in that boy. He reminds us a lot of you Paw. He is a smart one, for sure."

Lem grinned, and was proud to hear this talk, about his oldest son, Billy. He had heard this many times, from those who had been around his son; it was hard to miss.

Eli laughed, and said, "I hope he only caught the good parts of me, lots of me that he would not want to be like." Eli grinned and Billy blushed at the attention and looked at his feet.

Eli thought this boy *was* special, and he wondered if his grandfather Angus had looked at him, in this same manner.

Unbeknownst to the group, they had made plans that would change the lives of people for generations in the valley. They had no knowledge of fact, but only thoughts of supper, and seeing the rest of the family.

Although it was a cool evening, they ate outside under the chestnut tree, Jack and Becky joined the newcomers.

Newt and Lem were happy to see Jack. They had not seen him since his last visit to Georgia, before arriving back in Eli's life.

They all enjoyed good food and good company well into the evening. Although she enjoyed the company, Maggie was not a young woman and it would wear on her some, Becky thought so she volunteered their cabin for temporary quarters for Newt and his family, to help ease the congestion in the cabin.

Lem and his family would share the cabin with Eli and Maggie. Eli liked this because he wanted to learn more about Billy, he might just have plans for him.

Maggie and Eli settled down at the end of the day. Lem and family, being tired from the trip, had all settled into the beds. The floor of the cabin occupied with quilt pallets, occupied with MacGowans scattered around the cabin and loft.

Things became quiet and Eli and Maggie slipped out to the porch, Maggie, wrapped up in a blanked, and joined her and Eli hugged her close.

In the twilight, he could see the graves of his three children and his mother; he knew they were in a good place, and he would see them again. It *would* be a good time.

Eli felt at peace with God. Maggie was happy.

CHAPTER TWENTYTHREE
CHANGES IN THE VALLEY

The days blurred by into months and Becky's time came. Jack had been sticking close by Becky because of her condition. Not that he had any knowledge of babies, but he just felt at ease being close by.

The day arrived; Becky told Jack that it was her time. Jack, with a look of terror on his face, sent Newt's daughter Annie to fetch Maggie.

Maggie came as fast as her old bones could come, she wound across the trail, crossed the foot log over MacGowan Creek with ease and on to the cabin.

Maggie was not coming just for support to Becky, but her purpose was to deliver the baby. She had been on hand to deliver most of the children born into this valley. This was her calling she always thought.

Her grandmother had trained her in the art of child birthing in the years following her marriage to Eli. Maggie hoped to find one of her granddaughters, to share this knowledge.

Maggie arrived and in a matter of fact way, directed Jack and the young children to the front porch so as not to be in the way. Newt's wife Mary was there and Maggie noticed her fifteen-year-old granddaughter; Annie was still in the room.

"Annie, honey you need to go out, with the others." A look of disappointment, framed by her long auburn hair, swept across Annie's pretty face.

Mary said, "She wants to learn Maggie." Maggie smiled and asked, "Do you think you can take the sights, there will be some blood and lots of pain, Becky might do some screamin' too?"

Annie said, "I can take it Granny, I want to learn, I have prayed about this and talked to my mother, I can take it. I think this is my callin'."

Mary spoke, "she is a strong girl Maggie, and she can endure it, I think."

182

"Well," said Maggie, "if it is alright with you, Becky I reckon we can teach her some, about bringin' babies into the world."

Becky groaned a yes and said, "It is goin' to be here soon Maggie."

"Well," said Maggie, "let's tend to this baby."

Annie was all eyes and ears as she took direction from the saintly old midwife that happened to be her grandmother.

Maggie was proud to pass this down to someone because she knew she would not be able to do too many more, as she was getting to be an old woman.

Annie listened as Maggie showed her how to turn the baby's head and shoulders to make it easier on Becky. Becky screamed on a few occasions but Annie didn't falter from her concentration.

Maggie knew Annie would be the one as she watched her granddaughter deliver the first offspring of Jack Mankiller.

The baby arrived into this world quietly.

Maggie told Annie to take string and tie the cord in two places. They took a knife heated over a candle and cut the cord between the ties.

She asked for a clean cloth to place the newborn on, and told Annie to take care because the baby is slippery. They handed her to Mary to clean up as Annie and Maggie tended to the afterbirth.

Maggie patted Becky on the leg and said, "You did some good work here today, missy."

"So did you Maggie, I was glad to have you here, both of you," as she looked at Annie and Mary. She smiled a tired smile and said, "Can I see my baby now?"

Maggie took the baby and bundled it tightly in a clean blanket she had made for Becky, only last month. She handed the baby to its new mother and smiled.

Maggie said, "Let's get things cleaned up and let Jack Mankiller see his son."

Becky's face beamed as she saw her son for the first time. He had dark skin and a head full of black hair. She said, "He looks like his Paw, you think Maggie?"

"Yep, I reckon he does favor him some," said Maggie, "I think it is that same old toothless grin for sure." Becky grunted in pain as she laughed, Maggie apologized for making her laugh.

Maggie went to the door and said, "Jack come and see your son."

Jack cautiously eased into the dimly lit room, and saw his beautiful Becky with his son, in her arms. He paused to take in the sight he saw, thinking it was the most wondrous thing ever, his loving wife, holding his first-born child.

Becky smiled and said, "Come see your son, Jack" as she handed him to his father. Jack was not much for holding babies and he awkwardly took the young Mankiller and looked at him.

Jack said, "He ain't much to look at is he?"

"Well, I reckon that is 'cause he looks like you Jack," laughed Maggie.

"I reckon so," said Jack. "I think we will take him anyway, don't you Beck?"

Becky smiled and said, "Yes we will keep him, for the rest of our lives."

Jack said, "That might not be too long, if I have to wait through many more days like today."

"Me too," said Becky, "me too." They smiled at each other and Jack leaned down and kissed Becky on the forehead.

Maggie was proud for Jack and Becky, as well as happy about having a new student, in Annie, to pass down her traditions to.

"Somebody better send word to Eli, he'll want to know, "said

Maggie.

"I'll take him down to show him to Eli," said Jack. "*No!*" said Maggie "he can't be fannin' around outside for a few days, better let Eli come here Jack."

Mary said, "I'll go fetch him Granny."

Mary delivered the good news to her grandfather, and soon Eli MacGowan strode into the Mankiller cabin he had built.

Jack Mankiller stood grinning and presented his new baby boy to Eli.

Jack said, "ain't he a goodun' Eli?"

"I reckon you must be proud," said Eli, "he is a goodun' Jack, good as I ever seen. Becky you have done good with this one. He is a good-sized boy."

Becky smiled and said, "We have talked about a name, Jack and me, we settled on one, will call him Elijah Jack."

Eli said, "Well, that is a right good name," as he held him up to the window and presented him to the valley.

"Good people of the valley, meet Mister Elijah Jack," as the words left Eli's mouth the baby wet all over his presenter.

"That is just like a Mankiller to spoil things," laughed Eli. They all laughed.

It was a good day.

The days and months to follow were good too. Every day filled with hard work, good eating, praying, good rest, and much laughter.

As the sawmill equipment had arrived and was set up for operation; it was a sight for people to see. Nothing like this steam contraption had ever entered this valley.

Eli thought Newt and Lem could have charged a good price, to let folks get a look. It took a considerable amount of time for the boys to get the mill into operation, but it was truly something to see working.

Billy was growing into his role as a manager even at fifteen. He was fifteen in age only, forty in his ways and wisdom.

They could make short work out of the largest chestnut, pine or oak log. It produced fine boards to make the framing, siding, and floors for their homes at first.

Then they built a new school, church and even old MacAndrews separated himself from some of his money and built a new store.

This building was truly worthy of its name of MacAndrews Mercantile and General Store; he expanded his stock and carried just about anything you could find in Isaac's store in Calhoun.

The settlement was growing and new houses sprang up like mushrooms in nearly every hollow.

Timber bridges replaced fords on the larger creeks. This allowed one to come and go, even if the water was up after a rain.

Change was not something Eli MacGowan favored. He cherished his privacy but even Maggie was starting to encourage him to build a new house. Eli said, "A house, I have lived in a sturdy log cabin all my life and see no good reason to build a house."

He knew it was a matter of time until Maggie wore him down so he just gave in and told the boys to cut him out a house pattern and he would build a frame house.

Billy and Eli discussed the layout of the new home of the MacGowan matriarch and patriarch. Eli and Maggie had some input, but mostly listened in awe; to their young grandson explain what they would want.

He took pencil and paper and scratched out his plans for his grandparent's new house. He said, "First you will want the kitchen here, Granny, so you can see the valley through the window; and you will want the bedrooms here, and the front room here, as he explained the complete design."

When he was finished, Maggie smiled and said, "That is good Billy; build it that way, if it suits you Eli."

Eli smiled and said, "If it suits you Maggie, it suits me. We will build it this way."

He walked Maggie and Billy over to the site where he wanted their house built. He paced it off and said here, and here, and so on, to show the corners.

Billy said, "I have it in my head Grandpa, we will do you proud."

Proud they did. What a grand house it was. Starting with a porch that surrounded three sides of the house, it had water that was gravity flowed from the spring to the kitchen so Maggie only turned a spigot, and would have all the cool spring water she would need.

Billy had a pantry built for the canned goods and it was cool enough to hang hams. The pantry had a stone box built, with spring water running through it, to keep milk and butter cool.

Maggie could not believe this home; everything was easy for her now. Cooking and cleaning was easy, and the food was just a few steps from her kitchen. She had a big smile on her face, after they moved in, to the new house.

Billy convinced his grandparents to whitewash the house, Eli first thought this was just plain vanity, but didn't fight it, as he knew Maggie wanted it done, so it would be.

The days following, were great and joy filled times for the Clan MacGowan. Eli spent evenings teaching Billy how to play Angus' pipes, and he *was* a quick study. Eli remembered how he anguished with parts of his lessons, from Angus.

Billy seemed to grasp every lesson, and go with it. He was playing all the tunes Eli knew, after the first summer. Billy was playing the tunes much better than he had ever heard the tunes played, by *anyone*.

CHAPTER TWENTYFOUR
AMAZING GRACE AND AULD LANG SYNE

The following years Eli and Maggie enjoyed the company of their family. They enjoyed the new house and the company of Jack, Becky, and young Elijah Jack.

Many evenings Billy joined them, he would play the old tunes on Grandpa Angus' bagpipes, as Eli would try his best to fiddle in tune.

One evening Eli brought out the pipes. He stood on his porch of the cabin and filled the bag with air and started playing the old Scottish tune "Old Long Ago" or as Angus and Gullie would have said in the Gaelic word "Auld Lang Syne"; he did this to honor Angus and Gullie and his parents and children.

The sound of the pipes carried up and down the valley, on this crisp fall evening. Every person and creature living or dead, paused to listen. Every ear would hear this, and know that it carried the voice of every Scot who had fought for survival in Scotland; every Scot who had suffered the waves on the cold Atlantic journey, to come to this new land; and every Scot who fought and died, to help make this nation come to life.

This tune, played from the heart and soul of Eli MacGowan, a Scot.

This would be the last time Eli MacGowan would play the pipes of his Grandpa Angus. He turned to Billy and handed him the bagpipes.

Billy somewhat puzzled at his grandfather's actions asked, "what you want me to play Grandpa?" Eli said, "You take them with you son, they are yours. I give them with my heart, as they were given to me. Keep them from harm, and teach another generation of MacGowans to play, as I have taught you."

Eli had tears in his eyes, as he passed the bagpipes to his grandson. Maggie could not bear to watch; she went into the house and prepared for bed with a lump in her throat and tears in her eyes.

She knew the significance of Eli's actions this night. She knew that Eli had passed the torch to the next generation as his grandfather had passed it to him.

Billy and Eli talked into the night, before going to bed. Billy told his grandpa of his plans to go to college in Knoxville, next fall. The teacher had told him he knew all he could teach him here.

Eli thought how much Billy reminded him of Gussie, and wondered what would have become of his youngest son, had the Yellow Fever not cut his life short.

Eli watched as Billy rode his horse down the road to the settlement. His eyes, dimmed by age now, caused him to smile because he could not see past the barn anymore.

Eli patted old Rocky on the head and went into the house.

Eli tried to slip into bed without disturbing Maggie, but was unsuccessful; she rolled over and hugged Eli.

Maggie said, "You made that boy happy tonight."

"I know," said Eli, "I can still remember the feelins' I had, when Grandpa Angus gave those pipes to me. I was happy for the honor of having them, and sad that he would not play again. I knew his time was short, just as I know, my time is short, Maggie."

"Oh, Eli don't speak that, you still have years ahead of you."

"No Maggie I'll not see many more seasons pass, in the valley. I am near eighty years old now. I have watched Jack age, I know I am doing the same. We are old men."

"I hope Jack will be around to finish watchin' his son grow into a man, which is my prayer tonight," said Eli.

"Maggie I have lived a good life. I have had a *good*, long life, a good family, good livin', and you, my wife, have been all a man could ever expect."

"Why are you talkin' like this Eli?" asked Maggie. "I just want you to know that I am happy and thankful for my life. When I go,

I'll be with my family that has gone before me, that will be a grand homecomin' indeed" said Eli.

"Well, enough of this talk tonight, let's go to sleep," said Maggie as she curled up behind Eli, and was soon asleep.

Eli drifted off with the sounds of Maggie softly breathing. He smiled and was soon sound asleep.

Eli dreamed, this night, of reunion. He dreamed of his father and mother, of his children, of his grandparents. It was almost real, how they appeared in the dream, he thought.

Eli's mother hugged him and said, "Welcome home, son."

"We have been waitin' on you, son," said his father.

Eli hugged his three children Gwen, Mattie, and Gussie that had died from the Yellow Fever. They all were happy to see him. Gussie asked his father where he had been.

Old Dawg was even there, wagging his tail to meet Eli.

"What a dream," Eli said.

They all looked puzzled and said, "This is not a *dream*, you are with us now." Eli figured dying was on his mind when he went to sleep, and this was the result of those thoughts.

"Well, it is good to see you all, but I must go back to Maggie now." He closed his eyes and opened them; he was still in his dream. This is a fine dream, Eli thought, a fine dream indeed.

Maggie woke from her sound sleep, to the sounds of Rocky barking out in the yard. She eased from the bed over to the window, to see what the commotion was. She looked down the valley and could see Jack Mankiller, headed to the cabin.

She remembered Jack and Eli were to going to MacGowans Lumber today. She knew Eli had been up late last night, but thought she better wake him before Jack Mankiller saw him, in bed after daylight, and would think him triflin'.

She smiled and went to wake Eli. She paused, and observed how peaceful this old man looked, when he was sleeping. She thought how a clear conscience and a good soul lived within this old man, that she loved with all her heart. She smiled her sweet smile, and reached to wake Eli.

"*Eli, Eli MacGowan* better get out of bed, Jack is nearly to the porch." Eli didn't stir. She went to his side, and nudged his shoulder, no response. She shook him harder, still no response.

Maggie turned and went to the front room and sat in one of Eli's hand built chairs. She heard Jack as he stepped onto the porch. He opened the door, stuck his head inside, and said, "Mornin' Maggie is Eli ready?"

Maggie didn't move. Jack felt something was amiss, entered, and walked to Maggie. She was crying.

"Maggie, what's wrong, where's Eli? Is he *still* in bed?"

"He is gone Jack, Eli is gone."

"Gone where asked Jack, where is Eli gone?"

"Eli has passed on; he died last night in his sleep."

Jack felt a weakness creeping over his old body as he went to the bedroom, he nudged Eli several times, and having seen enough dead people in his day, he knew Eli was not with them anymore.

Jack sat on the bed beside his old friend and brother. Jack said, "Eli, go in peace, go in peace Gigage Gitlu. I'll see you in the next world, my friend."

Jack felt a goodly sized part of his life had left him. They had so much of their lives intertwined, he knew it would be a hard world without Eli MacGowan, in its midst.

He patted Eli on the shoulder, closed his eyes, covered his head with the blanket, and joined Maggie in the front room.

Jack said, "Maggie come with me to my cabin and stay with Becky."

"No, you go get the boys and tell them to come, and I'll get him prepared," said Maggie.

Jack said, "I'll get Becky and go tell the boys. Maggie wait until we get back." "No," said Maggie "I'll be fine with Eli. Jack just help me get him on the table."

Jack watched from the bedroom, as Maggie removed the breakfast plate and coffee cup, she had prepared for Eli, he fought the tears; he knew he would have to hold up for Maggie, so he prayed for strength to endure the day ahead.

Jack helped Maggie place Eli onto the table, hugged her and left, to finish this hard task that lay ahead of him. As he traveled the familiar path his burden was so heavy, this day, he wondered how he could ever finish this journey, this day.

He thought how many lives would be changed by what he was about to say. He thought it was a task that he wished he did not have to complete.

Jack arrived at his cabin, stepped up onto the porch and took a deep breath. He could hear Becky stirring around the cabin, cleaning the breakfast dishes. He knew he would have to tell her, so she could go be with Maggie. Jack could hardly think straight because of the dread filled his body.

Jack thought about how many times Eli and him had cheated death, figured they would have, and *probably should have*, met their death by a bullet, a hatchet, or some wild animal. He thought about how he would have never guessed Eli would die an old man, in his sleep.

Jack took a deep breath and stepped inside, Maggie smiled at him and said "Jack Mankiller, *what* did you forget?"

Her expression quickly changed, sensing the look of dread on her strong Cherokee husband's face. She questioned Jack in a tone that was almost fearful of the answer she would hear. "What is wrong Jack?"

Maggie felt the pain in Becky Mankiller's scream. It carried a thickness of its own, as it echoed up the valley, she knew that Jack had reached the cabin and gave Becky the terrible news. Maggie sobbed, thinking how the news of the passing of this old man, that lay before her, on her kitchen table, would cause so much sadness on this day.

Maggie took a deep breath, washed Eli, and placed his Sunday suit on for his wake. She felt at peace with his departure, and calmly finished his preparation. She had done this task for her dead children, and could remember how sad she was while preparing their young bodies. She had prepared Eli's mother and now she had lovingly prepared Eli, for his last journey from this world.

Jack readied to continue on his way, to give the sad news to Eli's sons and daughters.

Becky quietly said "take Elijah Jack with you Jack, I'll go to Maggie" and she did, as fast as her legs would carry her.

Up the trail, across the foot log on MacGowan Creek, past Eli and Maggie's old cabin to the front door of their house.

Becky paused before entering and wondered *what* she would say to Maggie. No words would come, so she just went to her friend, embraced her tightly for a good while, crying, no words would be necessary for a while.

Finally Becky spoke, "Maggie are you all right?" Maggie looked at her friend and said, "No Becky those days have left me. I fear I'll never be the same, I am not whole anymore, Becky, and will never be all right again, in this life."

Becky was numb with the pain she felt for Maggie, she just hugged her and they cried again, for a good while.

Maggie said, "Enough of this Becky, I'll not cry for Eli, he is at peace. He feels no pain in his old broken body. He now runs with Gussie and the girls, he's climbin' the mountains and ain't gettin' winded. He can play the pipes with his Grandpaw Gussie and the rest of the old Scots. I'll not cry for Eli. I'll not. He is at peace."

Meanwhile, Jack proceeded to the settlement he went to George's house first. He was the eldest son nearby, and Eli would want him to tell the others, Jack thought.

He saw George in the barn and went to deliver the words that he had rolled repeatedly in his head, during his ride from his cabin.

George knew something was wrong, from the expression on Jack's face. He wiped his head and with that Eli MacGowan grin, asked, "What is it Jack?"

"George I can't hardly get the words to come," his voice cracked.

"Jack, is somethin' wrong?"

"Yes, George, Eli is dead."

The words came from his mouth but Jack could not get used to the sound, it was a bad dream, Eli could not *really* be gone.

"Yes George, your Paw has died in the night."

George collapsed to his knees, the words striking his heart, took his breath. He could not speak and neither could Jack. Both of these burley men just stood in silence, looking at each other with tears streaming down their faces, finally George spoke. "Is Maw all right? How is she? Is she alone?"

Jack replied, "No George, Becky is with her and I need to get back, can you tell your brothers and sisters?"

George said, "I will and we will be there directly, go to Maw and Becky, your boy can stay here 'til things settle, if you want Jack."

Jack looked at his son and said, "Elijah Jack, stay here and we'll come for you later." The boy tied his horse and went into the house.

Jack said, "I had better get back now George." George nodded in agreement. Jack turned his horse and headed back up MacGowan Creek.

Jack's thoughts were with Maggie, his heart was breaking for her. He loved her, as a sister, and he hurt for her and himself as well.

He had always thought MacGowan would bury him but Eli was to be the first to go. Jack thought how things would be different; he would miss Eli, more than he could think, right now.

In his Cherokee reasoning, Jack thought, Eli has left me and I can't track him to where he is now, I reckon he will have to come and get me, when *my* time comes.

Back at the house, Maggie thought life was about the times one endures. She had endured much, so had this old man who lay before her, so had he.

Elijah MacGowan had a look of peace, Maggie thought. She kissed his lips and said, "Goodbye, my love. I'll see you in heaven."

They had the wake for Eli MacGowan at his house; there was a crowd there that night. It was a lively wake, music, food and drink. Maggie said to the group, "Eli would have loved to have seen this; he hated to miss a good wake." She thought the old Scots were there that night; she could feel their presence in the air. It was a good sweet feeling.

She was proud of the good people who traveled to send Eli on his way. She was hopeful that the youngins' in Watauga would get word in time to come by train. However, they could not wait too long they would have to bury him tomorrow.

They held Eli's funeral at the New Settlement Presbyterian Church. Eli was the center of attention; he would have hated that, Maggie thought. This was his church building she thought, he had quietly provided the lumber and materials to build the building. His sons and grandsons had sawed each board from chestnut logs cut from Eli's land. They hammered each nail and built every pew. Eli built the podium and alter by himself, thinking it required a master to finish such an important item of the church, for The Master's House.

The building had a quality that would rival churches in much larger towns. Eli said once that he owed this church building to The Lord, and to the good people of the settlement, who had stuck with him through the hard times. She remembered how thankful Eli was when the church was finished. He thought the church should be the nicest building in the settlement, and it *was!*

Maggie thought that Eli MacGowan was not dead, he lived in the timbers of this fine building, and his mark was on the building. His mark was on the faces of dozens of MacGowans who graced this building today. Yes, Eli was alive and well and here today.

The service was a somber one. Those in attendance shed many tears. They all had an Eli MacGowan story in their thoughts. He had done so much to help many people. He was always a giver, never asked any questions, just gave.

The time came to say goodbye to Eli. The pallbearers lifted his coffin to their shoulders and carried him to the wagon. They placed his body onto the rough boards and slowly proceeded to the MacGowan Cemetery, with most of the settlement in tow.

They rolled up MacGowan Creek past the homes of his sons, daughters, grandsons, granddaughters, and his best friend Jack Mankiller.

Maggie tried to remember what it looked like the first time she walked through the tall timber along this pretty mountain stream with Eli. She could see him grinning and knew he was a happy man.

"How things do change," she said to Jack and Becky, who were riding on the wagon with her.

They only nodded, as Jack said, "This change will be hard for us all," as he pointed to Eli's coffin in the back of the wagon. Maggie nodded with tears in her eyes.

The sun was going down as they reached the cemetery and the oldest grandsons reverently carried Eli to his grave. They all stood in silence for a while, then the sound of horse hooves clopping up the rocky road along MacGowan Creek, broke the silence.

Maggie watched, as her four sons from Watauga dismounted, and strode to her side. They embraced their mother not being able to speak, for the knots in their throats. There they were Elijah, James, William, and Jack MacGowan.

All of Eli's children were present to join with Gussie, Mattie, and Gwen, who slept beside their father, in their graves. Also in attendance, were near a hundred of his descendants and countless friends. The slopes of the ridge stood nearly full of those kind souls, who wanted to wish this good man a last farewell.

Maggie looked frail today, her eyes were sad. The usual spark was gone. Eli's passing had taken a large toll on her. She felt like falling onto the coffin and letting them cover her up with Eli.

She remembered telling Eli that only The Almighty could decide when we would die, but she hoped it would be soon. Life, without Eli, would be dark and empty for her, she thought.

All of Eli and Maggie's living sons and daughters surrounded their father's coffin. Isaac spoke first in his clear matter of fact baritone voice, of his fathers.

"We gather at this special place this evenin', to honor our father and our mother, who gave most of us here life. We honor our father in his passin', by our presence, he is proud, I know. We have all tried to follow the lessons we learned from our father. Those lessons have kept us well in our lives, we passed these lessons on to our youngins', as it was expected and it's clear we have done so. As we look around this place, we see the faces of good people, friends, and family. Eli and Maggie MacGowan, you have done well. We thank you both and hope we shall always hold your name high. I say Goodbye, my father, goodbye Elijah MacGowan. We shall surly see you in heaven, some day."

Jack Mankiller cleared his throat, and started to speak. "Eli, I do not have the words to say what really needs to be said. I only know what your life has taught me. I can't ever replace you, my brother. We *are* brothers, not by blood, but by choosin' and that made it special, I reckon. I would have given my life for you, any day; I know you would've done the same. We start our journey through the wilderness, when we are born. If we are lucky, we find people, to help us find our way. Eli MacGowan, you are my guide. I know I will be lost, most days, without you. Red, you taught me how to pray and showed me that God is real. For that, thank you, my brother. I thought that your stubbornness brought me here, but I know now, that God had somethin' in mind for me, and *that* is why, I was brought here. To find my Becky, to have a son, and place roots in the land you provided. Our journey together is done, in this world; I will keep a watch on Maggie, and keep her safe. I will see you soon enough, go in peace, Gigage Gitlu, go in peace."

Not many were able to speak after that.

Pastor Emmons cleared the sizable lump in his throat, knowing he had to speak some scriptures for Eli, he took a big breath and started with his service, "I would like to read some scriptures from The Holy Bible, the book of Ecclesiastes, chapter three. To everything there is a season, and a time to every purpose under the heaven: A time to be born, and a time to die; a time to plant, and a time to pluck up that which is planted; A time to kill, and a time to heal; a time to break down, and a time to build up; A time to weep, and a time to laugh; a time to mourn, and a time to dance; A time to cast away stones, and a time to gather stones together; a time to embrace, and a time to refrain from embracing; A time to get, and a time to lose; a time to keep, and a time to cast away; A time to rend, and a time to sew; a time to keep silence, and a time to speak; A time to love, and a time to hate; a time of war, and a time of peace. What profit hath he that worketh in that wherein he laboureth? I have seen the travail, which God hath given to the sons of men to be exercised in it. He hath made everything beautiful in His time: also He hath set the world in their heart, so that no man can find out the work that God maketh from the beginning to the end. I know that there is no good in them, but for a man to rejoice, and to do good in his life."

"Goodbye, Elijah MacGowan, you have surely done good in your life and we shall surely see you in heaven, my friend, Goodbye. Amen."

The boys filled the void in the ground that held the earthly remains of their beloved father. Maggie flinched and wept, as the hard clods struck the chestnut coffin that her sons had built for their father. Eli was gone, Maggie thought.

Off in the distance Maggie heard the pipes, it was Billy, and she thought, how sweet they sounded. Billy was piping his grandfather from this world, as had generations before him. He played his best renditions of "Amazing Grace" and "Auld Lang Syne."

Maggie thought Eli could surely hear the pipes and would be on his journey. She whispered, "Goodbye Elijah MacGowan, I'll soon see you in heaven."

The notes Billy played rolled down MacGowan Creek, for all to hear, it echoed up the eastern slopes of the Tennessee Valley to Watauga so Angus, Gullie, and his father could hear. The sweet sound cascaded up the Shenandoah Valley, crossing the mountains and valleys, where Angus and Gussie had pulled their handcarts. It carried out the Chesapeake Bay, crossing the cold Atlantic to the meadows and lochs of the Scottish Highlands. It faded into the soil of the ancient MacGowans, where it mixed with the hearts and souls of all the old Scots sleeping there.

The sound of the pipes caused them to stir a bit, knowing a fellow Scot had entered the gates of heaven to join them.

They all welcomed the arrival of their son from America, and returned to their slumber, with a wee smile on their faces.

-THE END-

ABOUT THE AUTHOR

Anthony Wilson was born and raised in East Tennessee. He has always had a deep interest in the history of the Scottish people who settled the lands of the Tennessee Valley. His ancestors moved to the valley almost 200 years ago. His knowledge of the valley and history helped him to write from the heart. It also allows him to base his fictional characters on a compilation of people he met.

During his life, he enjoyed writing, genealogy, golf, hunting, fishing, camping, and visits to the mountains and streams of his beloved Southern Appalachian Mountains of East Tennessee.

He retired from the U.S. Forest Service after 36 years as an Engineering Systems Manager. One highlight of his career was his involvement in the design and construction of the Ocoee Whitewater Center, the host site for the 1996 Summer Olympic whitewater events. His career at the Forest Service also allowed him to be a student of the outdoors, and gain a deep understanding of the relationship between man and nature.

He grew up hearing the fascinating stories told by his grandmother and many other "story tellers" of the past. His writing tells of an in depth personal knowledge of regional history and he intertwines that knowledge into his characters. His story will make you laugh, cry, and amaze you with the vivid picture he paints.

Made in the USA
Charleston, SC
26 September 2014